CALEB BLOOD

Caleb Blood was a man who'd seen too much bloodletting. He tried to forget, but despite the whiskey, his demons — past and present — wouldn't let him alone. All the things he should cherish were being stripped from his life. There was no option but to take up arms again. Once the guns were unlimbered, the death toll mounted and he faced so many enemies it seemed he had no chance of survival. When, he wondered, would the killing end?

P. McCORMAC

CALEB BLOOD

Complete and Unabridged

LINFORD
Leicester

First published in Great Britain in 2010 by
Robert Hale Limited
London

First Linford Edition
published 2012
by arrangement with
Robert Hale Limited
London

British Library CIP Data

McCormac, P.
    Caleb Blood.- -(Linford western library)
    1. Western stories.
    2. Large type books.
    I. Title II. Series
    823.9'2–dc23

    ISBN 978–1–4448–0988–6

Published by
F. A. Thorpe (Publishing)
Anstey, Leicestershire

Set by Words & Graphics Ltd.
Anstey, Leicestershire
Printed and bound in Great Britain by
T. J. International Ltd., Padstow, Cornwall

This book is printed on acid-free paper

To Sue and Chris Blood
for their unfailing hospitality

1

'Get them in the church. Get those sons of bitches inside.'

Wesley Harwinton, leader of the Jayhawkers, roared out his orders to his ragged band of raiders. His horse, a sturdy stallion, pranced about, made excited and nervous by the fevered yells of the big bearded man on its back and the smell of burning coming up from the town.

'Get them goddamn people inside that goddamn church.'

Harwinton was a great bull of a man with a voice to match. The raiders scurried around on their horses, herding the frightened townsfolk towards the church, a fine wooden building with whitewashed walls.

Caleb Blood was helping his comrades carry out his leader's orders. He tried to reassure the laggards as he gentled them along. At sixteen he was too young to join the regular army and so he had volunteered to ride with Harwinton's Raiders. As the war progressed they subsequently became known as Hard Winter's Raiders, for when they swept through a town or settlement they burnt and killed everything in their path, leaving behind a wasteland that no hard winter could quite match.

Caleb was not sure why the chief wanted the people penned up inside the church but, like his comrades, he was just following orders. He supposed his leader would want to do some preaching to the townsfolk when he got them in the church. Harwinton was in the habit of giving fiery speeches to his raiders. On the frequent occasions when he harangued his recruits he spoke to his men in the manner of a preacher, liberally quoting the Bible to illustrate his points.

Caleb was becoming more and more disillusioned with the actions of the raiders. The wanton acts of destruction and killings by his comrades seemed to the youngster callous and against all the principles of honourable behaviour.

Caleb had been fired up by the tub-thumping admonitions of the recruiting drives that saw most of his acquaintances going off to war. He too was desperate to join up and so, when the opportunity came to join Harwinton's band of marauders, he had jumped at the chance. Age had not been a bar to his recruitment.

Now he was gradually becoming disillusioned. His images of war were of glorious forays against an enemy who would fight him on equal terms. So far the band of raiders had done nothing but raid civilian outposts and kill ordinary people. He was beginning to feel a sense of shame at some of the actions of his comrades in arms.

When he had voiced his doubts about the righteousness of their behaviour someone had thought it fit to inform the leader. It had brought Caleb to the notice of the chief.

'This is a war we are fighting!' Harwinton assured the youngster. 'These civilians supply the Yankees with goods and services. Their sons take up arms against us. What do you think the rebels make of our tactics? I tell you what they think. They reason: 'Hell, I shouldn't be out here fighting in this stinking war. I should be at home defending my family.' Then Johnny Reb deserts and that's another gun that won't be shooting at our brave men on the battlefield. You see that, son? This is a necessary evil. The North must win this war. The Rebel soldiers are doing worse things to our people than what we are doing to theirs. By the Lord, we could not equal the atrocities committed by the Rebels against our poor suffering Northern folk. We are mere choirboys compared to them murdering scum.'

And now Hard Winter's Raiders had come to Perryville and the fires in the houses had started up already while the population was herded towards the church.

'Praise and worship to the good Lord,' Harwinton bellowed and his horsemen whooped and yelled and the inhabitants of Perryville were herded like cattle towards the beautiful white-washed church. The frightened faces of the women and the cries of the children were harrowing for young Caleb Blood and difficult to endure.

'It's all right,' he called out as his horse pranced about, unsettled by the screams and pitiful cries of the terrified citizens. 'Major Harwinton is just going to do some preachifying. You won't be harmed, believe me, we mean you no hurt.'

The people he was attempting to reassure were mostly women, children and the elderly, for all the young men had marched off to war, leaving their folk to manage the farms and keep the family home together while they were away. Now Hard Winter's Raiders had come and the villagers feared the worst. They milled around the doors of the church while the raiders yelled and chivvied them inside.

Eventually it was done and the last of the stragglers pushed through the large doors with the pieces carved into it so when it was closed a large cross was revealed.

More and more buildings in the town were going up in flames, and smoke from the burning houses began to darken the air.

'Get them doors shut,' Harwinton ordered.

The solid wooden doors of the church were slammed shut and the carved cross was revealed to the raiders. Men were racing up from the burning town carrying flaming torches. Harwinton waved the torchbearers forward.

'Get her burning, boys.'

Caleb did not believe it would happen. Right up till the first torch was thrown into the church he supposed the mock burning to be a warning to frighten the people of Perryville. The torches arced through the air, trailing burning debris and smoke and crashing through the windows.

'No!' he yelled. 'This ain't right!'

As he watched, horrified, a wagon was brought up and pushed against the front doors. Two torches sailed through the air and set it alight. The wagon was packed with kerosene-soaked hay bales, which caught immediately and sent a fierce sheet of flame licking at the doors, blackening the white wood and obscuring the cross.

The screaming from the burning church grew in volume. Suddenly a head and shoulders appeared at a window as someone attempted to climb out. Shots rang out and the head disappeared. The screaming inside the burning building was continuous now. Caleb spurred his pony towards his leader.

'Major, this ain't right. What are you doing? Stop this madness!'

The fanatical eyes were turned towards the youngster.

'Behold the wrath of the Lord. So shall all mine enemies perish in the flames of perdition. The Lord had judged these sinners and found them wanting. This is the fate of all enemies of the United States of America.'

Caleb grabbed the sleeve of the major and tugged hard, almost unseating his leader.

'Major, this is murder! Stop this madness!'

In a fury Harwinton drew his pistol and swiped at the impertinent youngster daring to question his actions. The barrel caught Caleb across the forehead and he reeled back, feeling the wet trickle of blood from the blow. Now it was Caleb who became angry.

'Let those people go!' he yelled.

Harwinton was fast. He whipped round and pulled the trigger. That was how he taught his guerrillas to fight; rapid fire, pouring a storm of lead at the enemy. Mostly the enemy were helpless civilians and as a rule were not organized to fight back.

As the major fired, his stallion nipped the young recruit's pony, causing it to jerk aside. The bullet that was meant to kill Caleb ploughed a bloody furrow along his forearm instead. In a reflex action the youngster pulled his own pistol and fired.

Caleb had been practising the fast draw to the amusement of his fellow raiders.

'When you meet up with Johnny Reb and he's shooting at you it's not a fast draw as will save you, it's a fast horse.'

Nevertheless Caleb had persevered with his practising and with sometime advice and help from the more experienced fighters had improved on his fast draw.

His bullet hit Harwinton in the chest. The big man swayed backwards, trying to hold his seat on his mount. The stallion, already excited by the activity and the flames and smoke of burning buildings, was thrown into a blind panic by the gunshots and bolted.

In the disorder around the burning church no one had noticed the gunplay between Caleb and the major. The raiders saw their leader in full flight and, believing him to be abandoning the town, they streamed after him.

As the raiders fled, the shrieks of the trapped people were growing less and less strident as they succumbed to the heat and smoke. Within a very short time Caleb was left alone in front of the burning church. Blood was streaming from his arm where Harwinton's shot had grazed him. There was blood also on his face from the blow on the head from Harwinton's pistol. For a moment only he became aware of the pain of his wounds while he stared up at the burning building. Then he urged his pony forward towards the church.

His mount was terrified and kept shying away. In despair Caleb abandoned the animal and ran forward to the fiercely blazing cart jammed in front of the doors. The body of the cart was well ablaze and the heat from the conflagration was intense. Caleb tried to shield his face from the fiercely burning hay. The roaring of the flames drowned out the last feeble shrieks of the trapped townspeople.

'I'm coming!' Caleb yelled and scorched his hands as he grabbed the shaft of the cart to pull it away from the doors.

'Goddamn!' he swore and danced around, waving his blistered hands in the air.

With a great whoosh like the bawl of a dying beast the roof of the burning building caved in. Caleb was showered with flaming embers. The heat from the huge fire was intense and drove him back. He fell to his knees and stared with horror at the inferno.

★　★　★

With a start he awoke, sweat soaking his shirt. He threw off the coverings and stared wild-eyed around the shack. Every time he fell asleep the terrible spectacle replayed in his dreams.

Whiskey! Only the whiskey helped and then only when he could get enough. Whiskey! He fumbled beside the bed for the bottle.

2

'Tell that lazy sonabitch boyfriend of yours to get his lazy ass up here. This place needs a good clean-up.'

The speaker was a large, florid man in a gold-embroidered waistcoat worn over a navy-and-white striped shirt and bow tie. Jess Jordan was the owner of the Horn of Plenty saloon. He scowled at the woman who at that moment was pulling a shawl over her bare shoulders.

Crystal Harkness was an attractive woman with long tresses of golden-brown hair and a full and lavish figure. She was dressed in a low-cut pink taffeta dress with a black sash pulled tight to draw in her waist and emphasize the full breasts and rounded bottom that made her attractive to the male customers. Wearing such a skimpy outfit the shawl was essential against the early-morning chill.

'Sure, Jess, I'll get him his breakfast and shoo him up here pronto.'

The saloon owner was still scowling at the woman while at the same time stroking his whiskers.

'Why you waste your time on that bum sure beats me,' he complained. 'A girl like you could have your pick of men.'

Which wasn't strictly true. Crystal was a saloon girl and though she had casual liaisons with men not many wanted to hook up with a painted lady.

'Aw, Caleb is all right. He's just sorrowing from some loss in his past. I reckon that's why he drinks, to forget. He won't talk none about it but I reckon he's running from some deep tragedy.' She stood there moodily, thinking about the young man she had taken into her home. 'Sometimes he mutters in his sleep and it's always the same. There's something about a fire and the women and children scream- ing. He thrashes about something awful and calls out like a lost soul in hell.

'Sometimes he just weeps. It breaks my heart to hear him. I try an' comfort him but he just lies there sobbing like a stray child as is missing its mother.' Crystal's face creased up in worry. 'You know what I reckon? He's lost his family in a tragic fire and he's the only one to survive. Or maybe it was his wife or sweetheart. Maybe he blames himself for what happened. I just don't know. He won't talk about it when I ask him. Just sits there looking like a whipped dog.'

The saloon owner cleared his throat. 'Hell, Crystal, it's just as I care about you and I hate to see you wasting yourself on that drunken bum. Kick him outta your cabin and when he has to stand on his own two feet and fend for himself he'll soon sober up and get a proper job. What sorta fella is content to sweep up and empty spittoons and run errands and let a woman keep him? It ain't natural. A young fella like that oughta be riding for some big ranch, herding cows or something useful. It sure beats me.'

'Don't be too hard on him, Jess. He ain't nothing but a lost child seeking his way home. Maybe he's found his home with me.' This last remark was said a trifle wistfully, then Crystal gave a short humourless laugh. 'A girl can dream, can't she?' She pulled the shawl close around her and headed for the door. 'See you tonight, Jess. I'll rouse Caleb and send him up here.'

With shoulders hunched against the morning chill Crystal walked towards the edge of town. She rented a tumbledown shack which she shared with her lodger, the man she had been discussing with the saloonkeeper who hired them both to work for him; Crystal to entertain the male customers and Caleb as a swamper.

'Caleb, you awake, honey?' Crystal called.

The shack was in poor repair. When it rained the roof leaked and when the wind blew it howled through the numerous cracks in the warped, ancient boards. At one time Crystal had used newspaper to cover the inside walls of the dwelling, but over time the paper had ripped and come away. Crystal tried patching over the gaps but it was a hopeless ongoing task as more and more of the paper gave way to damp and gravity and bulged out from the walls. The holes stretched and grew bigger, the fissures seemed to be leering, mocking at the woman's efforts to keep her little refuge tidy.

There was no answer to her query. Crystal went over and stared down at the man in the bed. She could not see his face for it was obscured by a jumbled mass of tangled hair. Caleb never visited a barber nor would he let Crystal trim his unruly locks. He rarely shaved but occasionally would hack with his knife at his beard.

'Caleb honey, you'll have to stir yourself. Jess wants you down at the Horn. We were busy last night and he needs you to clean up for him.'

She got a grunt for an answer.

'I'll cook you some breakfast, Caleb

honey. With something inside you you'll feel good.'

She rattled around the small stove, getting a fire going and pulling out a frying pan and putting on a coffee pot to heat.

'My old ma used to say eggs and bacon would set anyone up for whatever the coming day could throw at a body an' I reckon she was right, my old ma.'

She set two plates out and knives and forks and a couple of mugs on the table.

'Breakfast almost ready, honey. You better bestir yourself.'

There was a general upheaval and Caleb Blood groaned and rolled to the side of the bed. A hand reached out and groped around and came up with a bottle. Slowly he sat up, long straggly hair mostly obscuring his face. What little of his face could be seen was covered in dark fuzz. He pulled the strands of hair to one side, giving a glimpse of a pale, gaunt face and pressed the bottle to his lips. Crystal heard the gurgling and gave a quick distressed look in Caleb's direction.

'Honey, you think it a good idea to be drinking so early in the day like afore you even have breakfast?'

She served up the food and poured the coffee while Caleb fumbled for his boots. He was already dressed in stained, creased shirt and pants for he had fallen into bed last night and passed out without getting undressed. He picked up the bottle, shook it, then put it to his mouth again and drained the remainder. For a few moments he sat regarding the empty bottle.

'Need a drink,' he muttered.

'Breakfast's ready, Caleb honey.'

'Need a goddamn drink.'

Without looking at the woman Caleb swayed over to the door, fumbled with the latch and lurched outside.

'Caleb,' she called, but the door slammed and the man was gone.

3

They were surly men and dangerous. They rode into Musgrave and housed their mounts in the livery, then hired themselves rooms at the Horn of Plenty.

'How long for?' Jordan asked them as they signed the book and paid him.

The one that signed himself James Vance had a muscular build with powerful arms and shoulders. Underneath his hat he was bald. He had a stained bushy moustache that hid his hard cruel mouth. Jess Jordan suppressed the notion to step back a pace as he saw the cold blue eyes staring back at him.

'As long as it takes,' the man answered brusquely.

His companion was equally surly. He had a longish face covered in dirty stubble and a mouth that wore a perpetual sneer. The eyes of this man were just as hard and unfriendly. He signed the book as Tom Hardy. They ordered a bottle of rye and went to await the food they had requested.

'Them two mean sonabitches,' the saloonkeeper muttered, and out of habit he checked the Greener he kept stashed behind the bar.

The men kept to themselves for most of the evening and nursed a bottle of rye whiskey. Jordan tried to keep an eye on the two men but as the saloon filled up and he became busy they dropped away from his awareness. The trouble, when it came, was unexpected.

Caleb Blood, the flunky employed by the saloon owner, was collecting glasses and bringing them behind the bar where he was supposed to wash up and assist Bob Hopkins, the saloon's full-time barman.

Caleb Blood lived only for the alcohol he used to block the painful memories that blighted his waking hours. What money Jess paid him was spent on whiskey and the saloon owner guessed Crystal subsidized Caleb's alcohol habits also. Occasionally, customers feeling sorry for the youngster would buy Caleb a drink. Between all these sources of alcohol Caleb managed to feed his habit and was rarely sober enough to allow the demons that haunted him to surface.

The saloon was full and Jess Jordan was overseeing the running of the business. There were faro tables, a roulette table and a few card games run by housemen who worked for themselves but paid a percentage of their winnings to Jess. The bar was reasonably busy, the gambling was moderate, Crystal and two other women circulated amongst the customers encouraging them to buy drinks and enticing patrons upstairs to sample the delights of the flesh.

Caleb was kept busy collecting glasses and scrounging drinks from those patrons he knew had a soft spot for those more unfortunate than themselves.

The first Jess knew about the trouble

was the commotion in one corner of the saloon. He suddenly remembered it was in that location the strangers had been seated. There were yells and the sounds of a scuffle. Jess signalled the barman to watch over events and elbowed his way towards the tumult. Bob Hopkins, a tough old coot, reached beneath the bar and laid hold of the Greener and awaited developments.

The two strangers were on their feet with angry expressions on their faces. Caleb Blood was curled up in a ball on the floor and Tom Hardy was busy kicking the swamper. The customers nearest the disturbance were standing around eagerly watching the fight. In fact it was not a fight, it was a helpless drunk getting a vicious kicking. No one wanted to get involved with the two strangers everyone sensed were dangerous men.

'Whoa there, gents!' Jordan called as he took in the scene. He held out a placating hand. 'What seems to be the trouble?'

Mean eyes that seemed to burn red with anger turned towards the saloon-keeper.

'This filthy animal bumped me as I was taking a drink. I don't like whiskey soaks anywhere near me, never mind one that bangs into me and spills my liquor.' Hardy aimed another vicious kick. 'When I'm finished with this bum he won't be able to walk, never mind bash into anyone else.'

'Hell, he don't know what he's doing most of the time. He weren't meaning no harm,' Jordan tried to placate the angry man. 'It was just an accident.'

'It's the last accident for this dirty sewer rat.'

The speaker returned to his task of kicking the curled-up heap on the floor. With a sudden cry Crystal burst in on the scene.

'Stop it!' she yelled and flung herself protectively on top of Caleb.

'What the hell? Git away from that heap of shit!' Tom Hardy, deprived of his entertainment, shouted angrily.

'You've hurt him enough!' Crystal yelled back undaunted. 'You're just a bully and a thug!'

'You whorebitch! I'll show you what hurtin' is!'

Hardy suddenly pulled his pistol. Jess Jordan, seeing things getting out of hand, signalled his barkeep for help. At the same time he palmed a hideout gun.

'Enough, stranger, there's no call for gunplay. Like I say, it was a simple accident. Now put up that iron.'

Hardy turned his attention to the saloonkeeper. The gun he had been aiming at Crystal came round and was pointing now at Jordan.

'You wanna make me put it up? Just go ahead. Make your play.'

Jordan held his hands out from his body to show he was unarmed, the little hideout gun in his hand concealed from the gunman.

'Hell fella, is a spilled drink of rye worth getting into a shooting scrape for? You can have a bottle on the house if 'n you think you been hard done by. But put up that iron.'

At that moment Bob Hopkins, the barkeep pushed forward to stand on the other side of his boss. The shotgun was aimed directly at Hardy but both men at the table would catch part of the charge should it be necessary for the barkeep to fire the weapon.

A silence dropped in the saloon. Even the piano player had stopped. The tension built. Jess was watching the man he knew as Vance, who was behind the table knowing the barkeep would be aiming his weapon at Hardy, the one with the gun.

'Look fellas, it doesn't havta be like this,' Jess entreated. 'Have that drink on the house and let bygones be bygones. This is a peaceful town. Let's keep it that way. We ain't had a shooting in eighteen months. Don't spoil the run.'

'Tom! Let it drop!' Vance called out to his companion.

'Ain't no one spills my drink and no one points no gun at me neither!'

Hardy grunted, his gun still aimed towards the saloonkeeper.

'Tom, remember what we're here for. Don't spoil things.'

Those mean eyes burned with anger and a desire to inflict more damage. Tom Hardy wanted to kill someone. It was there in the mean eyes and the taut muscles of the face.

Jess Jordan could feel the sweat break on him. He was watching Vance, wondering whether he could shoot fast enough to down the man while his barkeep put a barrel of shot into Hardy. Hideout guns were notoriously unreliable at any distance. He needed to be up close but was afraid to move in case he initiated the very shoot-out he was trying so desperately to avoid.

The first barrel of the shotgun would be for Hardy, who already had his gun out. But who would be left standing when the gunsmoke cleared?

'Tom!'

Jordan could see the indecision in Hardy's eyes. The gunman was filled with a bloodlust that needed an outlet.

'Tom!' Vance called again, more urgent.

Hardy's eyes flickered sideways towards his companion. Slowly the tension drained from him and even more slowly, not taking his eyes from the saloonkeeper and the barkeep, he holstered his gun.

'You're lucky this time. Next time you sic a man on me with a shotgun you better make sure you put me down with your first shot, otherwise you're a dead man.'

He turned back to the table and grabbed up the chair that had been upset when the fracas had begun.

'Git that piece of shit outta my sight. If 'n I ever lay eyes on him again I'll shoot him like I would a mangy dog.'

The tension drained from the saloon-keeper.

'OK, Bob. Get behind the bar again. I'll serve these gents myself. Crystal, take Caleb home. He's to stay outta here for the time being.'

'Hang on, saloon man.' There was a

malicious glint in Hardy's eyes. 'How about this fine-looking whore taking me upstairs and making up for the upset that mangy cur caused me?'

'Crystal, you heard the man. I'll get someone else to take care of Caleb.'

Crystal was glaring at the saloon-keeper but he avoided looking at her. Hardy, with a leer, lumbered back on his feet and grabbed the woman by the arm.

'Come on, honey. You and me we got some lovin' to do. Vance,' he called over his shoulder, 'you comin' too, you don't wanna lose out on the fun.'

Jess Jordan watched the two men with the woman as they walked towards the stairs. There was something like regret in his eyes but also there was anger. He glared at the bundle of rags on the floor.

'Some of you men, help me with this piece of shit.'

4

With skilful use of whip and shouted orders Charlie Blood was busy reversing the wagon up to the boxcar. The old horse, well-schooled in harnesss, took short abrupt steps as it backed up while at the same time trying to look over its shoulder at its master seated behind him.

The boxcar had been shunted into a siding and was ready to unload goods for customers coming to collect with their wagons. Further up the tracks a train huffed and vented steam into the air like an idling beast waiting to be released.

'Hup! Hup! Caesar,' Charlie called. 'Hup! Hup!'

Man and horse were a team with Caesar often anticipating the rancher's wishes even before he voiced the commands.

'Steady boy, steady.'

'Charlie,' a voice called out. 'You're almost there — about another foot should do it.'

Charlie glanced over his shoulder at the boxcar attendant and waggled his whip in the air in reply. After a couple more steps Caesar stopped as the whip popped out and snapped above the animal's head. The whip never touched hide, Charlie using it only as a signalling device.

'How's that, Theodore?' Charlie called.

'Do right well, Charlie. Long as that hack of yourn don't start forward afore we git this wire loaded into that there wagon.'

Charlie hauled on the brake lever.

'Hell, old Caesar here'll stand like a statue till I give him the go-ahead.'

Theodore knew that quite well, but because the horse was so well-disciplined he liked to query it in order to see if he could rile Charlie. The rancher never did rise to the bait. With the wagon backed up to the open boxcar Charlie stashed his whip, jumped down from the driving-seat and walked back to help load up his delivery.

Charlie Blood was a tall man of medium build. He had regular features with a mouth that seemed ever ready to break into a smile. With quick, easy grace he swung up into the boxcar.

'Here Charlie, you'll need these.' Theodore handed him a pair of work-gloves. 'Hell, I never thought I'd live to see the day the range was fenced off.' Theodore spat out of the door of the boxcar, then turned and eyed up the rancher. The boxcar attendant was a middle-aged, chubby man with a belly straining at his leather belt. 'You sure you doing the right thing, Charlie, bringing in this here wire?'

Charlie was assessing the bales of barbed wire stacked inside the boxcar.

'It's the way things havta be, Theodore. A man's gotta protect his property. Them big ranchers think they own all the land and so do their cattle. I've had enough of sorting my cows out from herds allowed to roam where they like.'

'Houseman ain't gonna like this, Charlie.'

Mitchell Houseman was a cattle baron of the old school. His ranch, the Box MH, was the largest in the area. Houseman was into quantity rather than quality as regards livestock. He piled more and more cattle on to the range and as a consequence his herds were inclined to overrun other properties, which didn't bother Houseman but riled all the neighbouring ranchers.

Few ever dared make an issue of it, for Houseman was a notoriously dangerous man and the men he employed to run his ranch were equally mean and tough.

'Theodore, let's just get this here wire loaded,' Charlie said, preferring not to think what Mitchell Houseman might do or not do.

Charlie had thought long and hard about his decision to fence off his ranch but in the end reasoned his workload would become easier when he didn't have to make sorties out into the range and separate his own cattle from that of the Box MH. He suspected, but had no proof that some of his calves were hit with a Box MH brand when no one was around to witness. So he reckoned he would recoup the expense of the wire in the time saved and in hanging on to more of his own livestock.

Half an hour later the wire was loaded.

'Next stop, the store,' Charlie said as he stood in the doorway of the boxcar. 'I gotta get me a few groceries and, most important, I mustn't forget to stock up on candy.' He grinned at the attendant. 'Those two mites of mine look forward more to the delivery of that there candy than the return of their poor old hardworking pa.'

'Aw, git away with you! Those kids just adore their pa. How old they now?'

'Gale, she's six and Caleb he's going on five now.'

'Consarn it, whar's the time go, eh?

How's that lovely wife of yourn, Elvira?'

A shadow crossed Charlie Blood's face at the mention of his wife. He shook his head.

'Theodore, I sure as hell worry about Elvira. Sometimes she coughs enough to bust a lung. She tries to hide it but at times she brings up blood. Tells me not to worry but I sure do worry. I wanted her to take the train to Augury and see a doc but she tells me it ain't nothing an' gets angry if I make a fuss.'

'Probably nothing, Charlie. I imagine its just some flux that'll pass with the spring. You mark my words, Elvira will be out there helping with the chores afore you know it.'

'She tries to do that now but she just ain't fit. Times I see her holding herself and pale. It frightens me.'

'What about that brother of yourn? Him as you says you named your boy after, Caleb. Would he ever think of moseying over this way and giving you a hand?'

'Huh, Caleb!' After this dismissive

grunt Charlie stood in silent thought for a moment or two. 'Last I heard Caleb was over in Musgrave. I wrote him but never got no reply. I sure do worry about Caleb. He come outta the war a changed man. Took to drinking. I reckon whatever things he seen an' done in the war did something to his mind. He was wild afore he went in the war but he was never like that. Just drinking an' not caring about nothing.' Charlie sighed deeply before jumping to the ground.

'Some fellas is like that, Charlie. Drink takes aholt and they on a downward path. Nothing a body says will make no difference. They just hell-bent on killing themselves with liquor.'

Charlie turned and looked up at his friend. 'It weren't the whiskey so much. It were when he showed a yaller streak when he got in a row with Mathew Hecht, the Box MH straw boss. Hecht challenged him and Caleb backed down. Next day Caleb was gone. Now every time Hecht sees me he pokes fun at me about Caleb the Coward.' Charlie walked to the front of the wagon and climbed up to the driving-seat. 'I guess I'll mosey on down the store and get me that candy. I'll see ya, Theodore. Keep them bogies rolling, ya hear?'

'See ya, Charlie. I'll be back here next week. Mebby we can have a drink together. Give my love to Elvira an' those kids of yourn. I hope to see them soon.'

'Hup there, Caesar.'

The whip popped inches from the horse's ear and Caesar leaned into the traces. With the weight of the wire bales the wagon was heavy but the old horse dug in its hoofs and the vehicle rolled away from the railroad depot and into town.

5

Charlie Blood reined in his wagon outside the general store.

'Whoa there, Caesar,' he called and cracked the whip.

He tried to ignore the three cowboys lined up on the boardwalk watching the young rancher step down from his wagon. Still carrying the whip Charlie moved to the front of the wagon with a feedbag for Caesar. As he did so the men stepped down into the dust of the street.

'Blood.'

Charlie nodded in the general direction of the men.

'Howdy fellas.'

He slung the feedbag for the horse and the animal immediately began nibbling at the oats.

'I hope you ain't thinking to sling that wire, Blood.'

Slowly Charlie turned towards the men lined up in the street.

'Hecht, now what in the hell would I buy wire for if I weren't purposing to using it?'

'Not on this range you ain't.'

The man who spoke was Mathew Hecht, range boss of the Box MH, a big blond man with square broad face and wide cruel mouth. He was the man who had slapped Charlie's brother, Caleb, called him a coward and driven him out of town.

Charlie had burned with shame at his younger brother's humiliation but decided he was too busy running his ranch to get involved in fighting his brother's battles. The young rancher turned his gaze towards Hecht.

'Since when did you decide what a man does with his ranch, Hecht?'

'Ain't me as decides anything. Mr Houseman decides what goes on in this territory. He says no wire and when he says something then it becomes my bounden duty to carry it out.'

'You go back to Mister Houseman and tell him to go take a running jump at himself. No man tells me what to do or not to do. I ain't no ass-licking foreman as jumps every time his boss tells him to.'

Hecht's eyes narrowed and his hand strayed to the holstered gun at his side.

'You calling me an ass-licker, Blood? 'Cause if you are you'd better back it up with more'n just words.'

There was an open sneer on Charlie Blood's face.

'What you gonna do, Hecht? Gonna pull that pistol of yourn and shoot me. You're sure one brave man with a pistol in your hand and the two belly-crawlers as you need with you to back you up. Some day I'll catch you alone, Hecht, and then we can slug it out man-to-man, no guns, no back-shooters. Just you and me, Hecht.'

Sensing trouble brewing a small crowd was gathering to watch the confrontation. Hecht had been gripping the butt of his gun and when Charlie included his companions in his insults they too placed hands on weapons.

The straw boss was becoming angry at Blood's defiant and insolent words. He wanted to pull his pistol and beat the arrogant rancher into a bloody pulp. But he was conscious of the gathering townspeople and was also aware of Charlie Blood's popularity. He knew he had to tread warily.

'You're no better than that brother of yours. Caleb Blood crawled from this town his tail between his legs. It runs in the family. How long will it be afore you get out while you can still crawl?'

Charlie's face went white as the jibes struck home. He had resolved to keep his cool and not give the cowhands an excuse to cause trouble. But when the honour of a man's name was called into question he could but react in only one way.

'Take that back, Hecht,' he gritted out. 'Ain't no one call me yalla.'

'What you gonna do about it? I say as all Bloods thinks with their legs and runs when trouble comes their way.'

It was too much for Charlie. Almost without thinking the whip snaked out and the leather wrapped round Hecht's wrist. The straw boss had been gripping his pistol and when Charlie jerked on the whip Hecht's hand was wrenched forward yanking the pistol free of the holster.

Hecht snarled angrily as he was forced to step forward while his gun fell into the dust. Charlie Blood closed the gap between them and smashed his fist into Hecht's face.

The big man staggered back. Then, recovering quickly, he bellowed out a yell of rage and lunged at his attacker. The force of his charge pushed Blood back and they crashed into Caesar, who was wholly engrossed in the feedbag. The horse whinnied in alarm and tried to pull away from the struggling men. The distraught beast, still harnessed to a laden wagon, had nowhere to go and plunged about in fright.

Grunting and cursing the men

wrestled violently, each trying to throw the other. Their faces were inches apart, red with rage and effort. Though both men were about equal in height Hecht was the heavier man, bulky with muscle, while Charlie Blood was lean and wiry, though equally strong.

While the men grunted and strained for advantage Hecht's two men circled round looking for a way to help their boss. They could not get at Blood, for the men had now worked their way between the frightened horse and the hitching rail at the edge of the boardwalk. Charlie managed to hook his boot behind Hecht and topple the straw boss. The two men, still clamped together, fell with a dust-raising crash to the ground.

They rolled apart and immediately scrambled upright. Blood swung a roundhouse punch that landed on the side of Hecht's head. Ignoring the blow Hecht punched hard into the other man's midriff. Blood grunted and bent over under the force of the blow. A hard uppercut from Hecht straightened him again and he backed away, gasping air back into his lungs.

Hecht remorselessly bored in, his fists hammering, left right, left right. Charlie Blood gave way under the onslaught, trying to block the jabbing fists. He feinted another roundhouse and Hecht, anticipating the swing, brought up his arms to block. Blood changed tack and brought up his other fist in a vicious uppercut. He was lucky; his fist striking low caught Hecht in the throat. Hecht gagged and instinctively tried to protect his damaged gullet. Now he was the one backing away.

Charlie Blood bored in, hammering relentlessly at his opponent: chest, midriff, and face with Hecht desperately trying to protect himself from the ferocious barrage. And Blood was definitely winning the fight. That lucky strike from Blood, which had caught Hecht in the throat, was causing the straw boss problems as he gasped for oxygen. That was when Hecht was rescued.

His two companions had gotten behind the battlers. Both had drawn their pistols. Once within range it was a moment's work to smash the barrel of a Colt into the back of the rancher's head. Charlie's head jerked forward under the blow. The second cowhand used the butt of his Colt to hit the rancher again in the side of the head. The first blow dazed him, the second took the starch out of his legs and he went down.

'Goddamn bastard, Blood!' Hecht snarled hoarsely as he gazed down at the dazed rancher.

He kicked the downed man viciously in the side. Charlie Blood groaned and tried to roll away from the punishment.

'Gimme that Colt!' Hecht yelled. He snatched the pistol from the cowboy's hand. 'Nobody hits me and gets away with it. Let's finish this now!'

He was lining up the gun when a voice roared out: 'Enough! Put up that gun!'

Hecht hesitated.

'Mathew!'

Hecht knew that voice. He paused and looked up, uncertain. His boss, Mitchell Houseman, was standing large as life on the boardwalk, glowering at his foreman.

'Put the gun away.'

Slowly Hecht stepped back and handed the gun to the man from whom he had snatched it a moment ago. He let his empty hand fall to his side and stood scowling at his boss. Mitchell Houseman flicked his head. The Box MH men moved back and stepped down from the boardwalk.

'He started it, boss,' Hecht growled.

'Get down the livery. Wait there for me.'

Hecht recovered his gun from the dirt and they went — surly and still angry, but they went just the same.

Charlie Blood was sitting up now and staring dazedly at the boss of the Box MH.

'I just saved your hide, Blood.'

Mitchell Houseman was a bull of a

man. Well into middle age he had a powerful frame with a face like weathered stone. Right now his mouth was drawn down in a grimace as he stared at the young rancher. He leaned over and held out his hand as if offering help. It was all for show. People were watching and he was canny enough to play to the audience. His words held no warmth.

'Listen to me, Blood. Today's bother is only a taste of what's to come. If you string that wire I won't be able to save you next time. Cowmen don't like wire. Every rancher around here will be your enemy. So be warned, Blood. You don't want to end up like that cowardly brother of yours and be run outta the territory or, worse still, make those kids of yours into orphans.'

6

The coughing was getting worse. Charlie could sense a change in his wife's condition and he was scared.

'Elvira, drink this. I made you some milk and honey,' he urged her gently.

She nodded and tried to drink but the coughing started up again and he had to hold the cup to keep it from spilling. When she caught her breath again she smiled weakly at him.

'Poor Charlie, I'm more bother than I'm worth.'

He did not have to make answer, for she went into another spasm of coughing.

'Rest easy, darling. I guess I'd better go for the doc.'

Elvira shook her head in protest. 'No need, Charlie. A day or two and I'll be as right as rain.'

She is beautiful, he thought, as he

looked down at her. Even with this illness she is still beautiful.

He stroked her hair, so long and black. Her face was narrow, with full sensual lips and smooth, olive skin. She closed her eyes, content to let him comfort her, and under his gentle stroking she fell asleep. He rose from her side and went into the kitchen. The children were at the table working with flour and milk. Gale looked up as her father entered.

'Look, Pa, I'm making biscuits. You can have them for supper.'

He smiled as he examined the dough she had prepared. 'Dang my hide if'n that don't look as good as your ma makes.'

'Oh much better, Pa. You'll see.'

Her brother Caleb was kneeling by the stove, feeding in small logs.

'Is Ma real sick, Pa?' Gale asked shrewdly.

'She is a bit but she'll be better soon. Look, I'm going into town to get some medicine for her. Doc Burrows told me to come and see him if your ma didn't stop coughing. You two hold the fort till I get back. I'll be as soon as I can with the medicine for Ma and she'll soon be on the mend.'

The young, old eyes looked up at him. 'Sure Pa, I'll take care of things. I'm six now.'

'I'm six too,' Caleb chimed in.

'No you're not, Caleb,' Gale interjected. 'You're five.'

'I'm nearly six, ain't I, Dad?'

'You're not to say ain't, Caleb. Ma tells you off for that.'

Charlie grabbed his hat and left his children busy arguing and cooking supper and went and saddled up for the ride into Newtown to fetch medicine for his sick wife.

The trip to town was uneventful. Charlie made a detour to admire the shining strands of wire he had been stringing along the boundaries of his ranch. He was pleased with his progress and also slightly puzzled there had been none of the expected backlash from the Box MH.

'Hell, that beating I gave Hecht musta scared them MH hellions away. They know now I ain't the sorta man my brother Caleb is. I'll fight back if they give me any trouble.'

It was late afternoon when he got to Newtown. He found Doc Burrows and obtained medicine for Elvira.

'Charlie, I'm just going down the Silver Sphere. Won't you join me for a drink?'

'Hell, Doc, I should be getting back to the ranch. I left Elvira sleeping and the kids were baking cookies for supper.'

'That Gale, I reckon she could run that house of yours on her own. Come on, Charlie, one drink won't do any harm. You need to relax. All work and no play makes Charlie Blood a dull man.'

It was late when Charlie eventually decided he'd had enough of the doctor's convivial company. The good feeling engendered by the alcohol began to sour and Charlie's woes soon surfaced.

50

Dusk was settling over the land as Charlie Blood rode back home, feeling guilty for being away so long from his family. The bottle of medicine was tucked inside his shirt pressing uncomfortably against his belly as if accusing him of neglect.

An immense sadness overwhelmed Charlie as he thought of his beautiful wife and the sickness that wore her down day by day. Doctor Burrows would not predict how the illness would progress but would only tell Charlie to keep giving the medicine.

'Hell, maybe I should send Elvira back East to see one of those city doctors,' Charlie said, thinking out loud. 'I could sell last season's calves. They're fattening up nicely and should fetch a good price. I won't miss them that much and now the wire's going up I'll be able to keep my batch of calves instead of being drawn off by them thieving Box MH rannies.'

Movement up ahead interrupted his musings. He frowned and peered hard

51

into the deepening dusk.

'What the hell . . . '

At first he thought it was stray cattle milling about at the wire, for the movement was at his boundary where he had been erecting his fencing. Then as he drew nearer he saw it was horses and men. A grim suspicion was growing in his mind.

'My goddamn wire fence.'

He dug his heels in and the horse bounded forward. His suspicions were confirmed as he saw a section of fencing being dragged free by a mounted man using a rope. There were three men busily destroying the wire fence that had taken days of hard labour on the part of the young rancher.

'You blaggards!' Charlie yelled as he bore down on the group. 'What the goddamn hell you think you're doing?'

The raiders, taken by surprise were wheeling their mounts around to face the charging horseman. Before they could respond Charlie was upon them.

As he came up to the first man he lashed out with his fist and caught him a wild blow in the face. The rider yelled as he was punched and reeled back in the saddle. Charlie did not let up. He pulled his mount around and punched hard and straight again catching the other rider on the side of the jaw. This time the man lost his seat and toppled to the dirt.

Charlie was mad as hell and turned towards the remaining two raiders. He immediately recognized the foreman of the Box MH.

'Hecht! I should have known. Skulking around in the dark like the coyote you are.'

Charlie kicked his feet free of his pony as he urged it forward and as he came level with Hecht he launched himself off his mount and crashed into the foreman. He wrapped his arms around the man as they both went over the rear of Hecht's mount. Charlie was on top as they landed and the impact knocked the wind out of Hecht. Anger was driving Charlie and he rose above his captive and drove his fist hard into the man's face.

'You goddamn lily-livered coward!' he yelled. 'Sneaking round at night destroying my goddamn fence.'

Charlie was pounding his victim as he spoke, matching his words with punches. Dazed by the initial fall from his horse Hecht was helplessly trapped beneath the insensate rancher and was unable to protect himself as the youngster hammered him. He struggled vainly against the weight of his attacker while the punches rained down.

'Help me!' he managed to yell.

The one cowboy who had remained mounted rode his horse alongside the struggling men. He had drawn his rifle and holding it by the barrel he swung with all his force at the rancher. There was a dull thud like the sound a mallet makes as it hammers home a wooden peg. Charlie arched away from the rider, his senses reeling. His attacker was merciless. He swung again at

Charlie and the stock of the rifle splintered as it hit for a second time. Charlie made a peculiar mewling sound and toppled sideways. His arms and legs were moving feebly as he tried to scramble away from the man with the rifle.

Hecht rose to his feet, drew his pistol and smashed it down on Charlie's head.

'You bloody mad bastard, Blood. That's the last time you hit me.'

Charlie lay in the dirt making no movement.

'That'll teach you to mess with Matthew Hecht. There'll be no wire on this range, you hear? Every time you put it up we'll come along and tear it down.'

Charlie Blood made no reply. He lay motionless in the dirt while the men who had destroyed his fencing rode away into the night. Not only had they destroyed the fencing but they had also destroyed the life of the young rancher. The Blood children were without a father and Elvira Blood was now a widow.

7

Vance and Hardy were checking out of the Horn of Plenty.

'Hope you enjoyed your stay, gentlemen?' Jess Jordan queried, hiding his relief that these particular guests were departing.

'I stayed in better places,' Hardy said. 'One fleapit is as good as another.'

Vance said nothing, content to give vent to a meaningless grunt. Once mounted the unsavoury pair rode down the main street of Musgrave giving the bank one valedictory glance.

'What you think?' Hardy asked. 'The bank should be a pushover.'

'Yeah, they ain't never had a raid afore. When we hit it they'll be running round like chickens with a coyote loose in the henhouse.'

At the outskirts of town Hardy nodded his head towards a ramshackle cabin. 'That's where that lousy drunk hangs out. The one as spilled my whiskey. When we come back I'm gonna finish what I started and shoot a few holes in that good-for-nothing bum. I reckon I'll be doin' this town a favour killin' that worthless piece of shit.'

Lance looked sideways at his partner. 'Hell, Tom, I don't know what makes you so mean. That bum ain't worth a lead nickel never mind a lead bullet.'

'I just like to kill things.' Hardy gave a mirthless laugh. 'I see a bug crawlin' and I squash it with my boot. That worthless bum crawls around this town and it's time someone squashed him into the dirt.'

'Come on, let's get back an' tell the gang the good news. In a week or so we'll be livin' the highlife. Mind you, one thing this rotten town had that I was gettin' used to was that Crystal gal. Reckon I could persuade her to come with us when we ride away with the money from that bank.'

It was Hardy's turn to look askance at his partner. 'Hell James, there's plenty more like that Crystal. Every town we hit has a Crystal.'

'Yeah, I guess you're right at that.'

The two outlaws passed beyond the town boundaries and were soon out of sight of anyone who might have been observing their departure.

As James Vance and Tom Hardy left Musgrave a wagon driven by a young woman passed them on the road. The outlaws gave the wagon a brief inspection. The wagon itself was of no interest but the woman sitting in the driving-seat invited attention. Even though painfully thin she was an exceptional beauty with long dark hair. Beside her on the driving seat sat two small children. The men touched hats and eyed up the woman but she barely acknowledged the greeting.

The wagon passed and the outlaws continued on their journey, wondering what a pretty young woman was doing driving all alone with two kids.

As the wagon progressed towards Musgrave the woman began coughing. Turning her head away from the children she coughed long and hard. She pressed a cotton pad against her mouth to contain the crimson stain that leaked from her lips. Wearily she leaned against the backrest and stared ahead, seeing the town marker coming into view.

'Look, Musgrave. We're nearly there, children. That's where Uncle Caleb lives.'

The youngsters stared solemnly at the lettering on the sign but remained silent. The shock of their father's death had left its mark upon all the family and they were still coming to terms with the brutal reality of life without a husband and father. Their whole lives had been turned upside down. Now coming into a strange town to face an uncertain future the bereaved family drove into Musgrave with a certain amount of apprehension.

The wagon trundled past the livery

stable and a saloon and various stores before eventually stopping at the general store and post office. Exhausted by the effort of getting this far Elvira stayed where she was for some time, gathering her reserves of strength. As she sat there a woman approached along the boardwalk.

Crystal Harkness was walking back from the Horn of Plenty to the shack she shared with Caleb Blood. She had not seen much of Caleb in the last few days, for the two guests at the saloon had monopolized her time.

Pandering to the men had been distasteful but Crystal had no choice. It was the nature of her job and she was long resigned to taking the good with the bad. She saw the exhausted-looking woman in the wagon and, being Crystal, the good Samaritan, she did not pass by but stopped and asked if she needed help.

Elvira smiled gratefully. 'Indeed. Perhaps you could you tell me the whereabouts of Caleb Blood? We have corresponded in the past and it has always been via the post office. I was about to go inside and enquire.'

'Caleb, why yes, I am on my way there now. Could I enquire as to why you seek Caleb?'

'I am a close relative and come here seeking his help.'

Crystal nodded her head, thinking of the pitiable creature that was Caleb Blood and wondering what sort of aid he could give this young woman. As she stood speculating on this Elvira started coughing and though the young woman turned away the saloon girl saw the flecks of blood appear on the woman's lips before she could get the stained cloth to her mouth.

'I'll go on ahead and see if Caleb is about. If you turn your wagon around and follow me back to the edge of town I'll watch out for you and show you the cabin he and I share.'

If Crystal expected any reaction to her revelation that she lived with Caleb she was disappointed. Elvira merely smiled wanly and nodded her thanks. Crystal continued on her homeward journey. She found her lodger sprawled on the bed in his usual dishevelled state.

'You bring me any whiskey?' he asked.

'Caleb, there's a woman with a couple of kids has come avisiting.'

Caleb's face turned towards her. She assumed he was staring at her but could not make out his face beneath the tangle of uncombed hair hanging like camouflage, hiding him from the world.

'Woman . . . visiting . . . I . . . you . . . ' It was obvious he could make no sense of this news. 'What the hell you on about?'

'I guess the wife you run out on has tracked you down at last.'

There was a tinge of maliciousness in Crystal's tone. She was irrationally jealous of this woman from Caleb's past. Nevertheless, she was listening for the sound of the wagon and went outside to guide the strangers to the cabin.

Caleb, seeing she had left her bag on the table, rose from the bed and searched for the whiskey Crystal invariably brought him. There were voices and steps outside. Caleb uncorked the bottle, lifted it to his mouth and took a long draught.

'Aaah . . . ' he sighed.

He was about to take another drink when the door opened and a dark-haired, pale young woman stepped inside. Immediately she began to cough. Caleb stared at her. There was more movement at the door and Crystal entered, ushering two young children before her. The children clustered around their mother shyly clutching at her skirts. The only sound in the little shack was the harsh sound of a young woman coughing up a storm.

Crystal was about to leave and let Caleb sort out his relationship with the young woman but compassion won and she moved alongside Elvira and took her arm.

'Please take a seat. I'll get you a drink.'

The little group moved forward,

Crystal guiding the woman and the children still clinging to their mother and staring wide-eyed at the strange man with the tangled mass of untamed hair and shabby clothing. Crystal got the woman seated and went to the stove to get some fire going.

Caleb was standing by the table, the uncorked whiskey bottle in his hand.

'Elvira . . . ' he looked towards the door, expecting his brother Charlie to follow his family inside. 'What has happened?'

8

Elvira turned to Crystal. 'Would you do me a favour and take my children outside a moment?'

'Sure, honey. Come on you fellas. There's a big store down the street has so much candy they're selling it to young children.'

Gale and her brother Caleb, lured by the promise of a treat, went with Crystal. Elvira started coughing again.

'Charlie's dead,' she managed to gasp when she caught her breath.

Caleb slowly sank into a chair on the other side of the table from Elvira. 'Charlie dead,' he whispered. 'That can't be.'

He stared across at his sister-in-law. Her eyes were hollow-ringed, her face pale and drawn. Mechanically he raised the bottle of whiskey and took a long slug.

'What happened?'

Elvira told him between bouts of coughing. 'It got later and later and then Charlie's horse came home. I knew then. I hitched up the buggy and drove towards town. He was lying by the fence he had been working on. The fence was all torn down.'

She began to cry then — great racking sobs that shook her frail body. Caleb didn't know what to do. He wished Crystal would come back. He felt helpless and adrift with Elvira sobbing and the image of Charlie lying in a field killed for putting in a fence.

'Weren't no call to kill Charlie like that. He was a good man. Who done it?'

She shook her head. 'Nobody knows, or nobody's telling.'

'What about the law? Maybe they'll find his killer?'

'Sheriff LeMoyne says he's investigating. He reckons it was rustlers killed Charlie. I got the impression he's not too bothered. Didn't even raise a posse to track down the killers.'

'You think it was rustlers?'

'Maybe; all I know is Charlie had a fight in town about a month ago with some of the Box MH men. Came home all bust up. It was over the delivery of wire he had just picked up from the railroad. They told him if he put the wire up they'd tear it down.'

Elvira fell silent but then started coughing again. Caleb looked down at the whiskey bottle he had opened just before Elvira had come into the shack. He took another slug but it didn't do any good. The pain of what had happened to his family was still there.

'Elvira, you don't mind me asking, why come here to Musgrave?'

'Caleb, we had nowhere else to go.'

'But the farm and all — what's happened to that?'

'After the funeral there was riders coming around at night. There was shouting and hooting and noises. Some nights they fired shots. I tried to watch out for them with the rifle but I never had the strength to stay awake. I was frightened they would hurt the children. As it was we were all in a state after Charlie's death. I couldn't take no more, Caleb. I had to get out. I didn't know where else to go.'

Charlie wished Crystal would come back. He felt helpless and adrift and he sank more whiskey, but it wasn't working.

'You want to lie down, Elvira? You look plumb wore out.'

She nodded gratefully. 'I guess.'

She struggled to her feet and Caleb felt bound to come round to her side and help her to the cot.

'I'm sorry, Caleb,' she said weakly. 'I had no one else to turn to. I was worried 'bout Gale and Caleb.'

She lay back and closed her eyes. Caleb noticed a clot of dark blood inside her nostril. He turned away and went back and sat by the table. Periodically he tipped the whiskey bottle to his mouth and drank. He was numbed with the thought of his brother being killed for putting up a fence. He shivered.

'Charlie, why are you dead and I'm still alive?' he muttered. 'It ain't right. Why didn't the good Lord take me instead of Charlie?' He gazed mournfully at the whiskey bottle, listening to the bubbling sound of his brother's widow breathing. A great fear gripped him. 'It ain't right. What good can I do? I clean floors and wash glasses down the Horn of Plenty. Elvira shouldn't have come here.'

The door opened and his niece and nephew stepped inside followed by Crystal. They were clutching small paper bags of candy. For a moment their eyes showed panic when they did not immediately see their mother.

'Where's Ma?' Gale asked, her voice small and frightened.

'It's all right, Gale,' Crystal assured the little girl. 'She's just lying down. I expect she's tired after the journey.'

The children edged warily past their strange uncle and clustered by the cot staring at their mother.

'You got your candy, I see,' Elvira

said in a weak voice barely above a whisper. 'Mummy's just going to rest for a little while. Uncle Caleb will look after you.'

Caleb heard the words with something like panic in his breast. He stared up at Crystal, his eyes pleading for help.

'Come on, kids, I guess you must be hungry. Seeing as you've not eaten your candy yet, your Auntie Crystal will make you some porridge with honey for breakfast. Then you can tuck into your candy.'

They stood shyly by their mother's bed and stared up at the two adults.

'Caleb doesn't like porridge.'

As his sister made this observation little Caleb burst into tears.

'I want my daddy,' he sobbed.

Elvira tried to sit up to comfort her children but was too weak to make the effort and fell back in the bed. Her coughing filled the little cabin echoing and sounding like hell to the listeners.

'That ain't no problem, Caleb. You tell me what you'd like for breakfast?'

'Candy,' he asserted.

Crystal laughed. 'Well, Caleb, why don't you just sit down by your Uncle Caleb and eat your candy. When I was a little girl I didn't like porridge either but I ate it anyway cos my ma told me it would make me grow up strong and tall. You can always tell me if you want anything after you finish your candy. Now what about you, young lady? What do you want for breakfast?'

'I want biscuits and molasses, please, Miss Crystal?'

'Now there's a girl after my own heart. Biscuits and molasses it'll be. Maybe you can help me with the mix. I ain't much good with this cooking business.'

Gale moved forward. 'I can make mighty good biscuits. I used to make them for my daddy . . . ' She blinked as she realized what she had said. 'My daddy was killed by bad men. Then they came and tried to kill us too. But Ma took us away. We're on our way to visit Uncle Caleb. Ma says he's my daddy's brother. We're going to live with Uncle Caleb. She said Uncle Caleb would take care of us.'

With a strangled cry Caleb grabbed the bottle from the table and stumbled to the door, wrenched it open and disappeared outside. There was silence in the little shack after the door banged to.

'What a funny man, Miss Crystal,' Gale said. 'Is he your husband?'

9

Life in the little shack would have been trying but for the extraordinary efforts of Crystal to make things as pleasant as was possible under the circumstances. Three adults and two small children living in a tiny one-room shack would have been unbearable, especially with one adult seriously ill. The journey to find her brother-in-law had torn the under-pinning out of Elvira and she was so weak she hardly left her bed.

Some long-buried instinct of motherhood surfaced and Crystal watched over the children like a mother hen with her chicks. The wagon the Blood family had arrived in was parked at the side of the house. This became an extra room utilized by the children.

'This is your magic cave,' Crystal explained to them. 'When you enter the magic cave of Obsidian you are safe from all the nasty things of the world. The bad men who chased you and your ma from your home don't know about this place. They won't be able to find you in here.'

Caleb spent as little time as possible with the family, even going so far as finding a bed at the livery stable. Marty Sandford, who ran the livery, was almost as fond of his liquor as was Caleb. From time to time Caleb would stagger back to the overcrowded shack to collect whatever whiskey Crystal would have procured for him, then it was back to the livery and oblivion.

On one particular occasion he found the shack deserted, or so he thought till he discovered Elvira weak and bedridden. He felt uncomfortable whenever he had to deal with his sister-in-law. Mumbling that he had forgotten something, he was about to retreat when Elvira raised herself up from the bed and beckoned him to her.

'Caleb,' she called weakly.

Reluctantly he turned and made his

way to her bedside.

'Can I get you something, sister? Perhaps a drink?'

He looked down into her face and was shocked by the way her eyes seemed to have sunk deep inside her skull.

'Caleb, you have been avoiding me. Are you ashamed of me?'

'I . . . I . . . it . . . I have been trying to leave space for you and your family. This place is so small — too small for us all.'

'You resent me coming here.'

'No. You are welcome. But it is not my decision. This place belongs to Crystal. I have nothing to give.'

'She is a good woman, Caleb. Because I am ill she has taken on the role of mother to my children. As well as caring for Gale and Caleb she takes care of me also.'

Exhausted by her efforts to talk she lapsed into silence. Caleb crouched by the bed, made uneasy by this intimacy. She was quiet so long he thought she had gone to sleep. But suddenly she spoke again.

'What has happened to you, Caleb?'

He did not answer for he knew not how. Instead he rose to his feet. 'I have to go now.'

'Don't go, Caleb. Sit with me a while.'

Not knowing what else to do he sank back on the floor and sat staring at his boots. For the first time he noticed how scuffed and dirty they were and wondered briefly how he had allowed that to happen.

'We were close once, you and me, Caleb. I thought I had found a younger brother in you and had a belief you were fond of us also, or was that an illusion?'

'I . . . things happened . . . I changed . . . '

He broke off, unable to speak about past events that had warped his life — dark memories of the horrors in which he had participated in a war that he still did not fully understand.

She reached out to him. Tentatively

76

he took her hand in his. In spite of the heat in the small cabin her hand felt cold. It lay pale and thin against his palm.

'What happened, Caleb? What happened to change you from the sharp young man to the creature you are now? You know Charlie and I loved you, but you turned us out of your life.'

He said nothing, seemingly mesmerized by the pale white hand lying so delicately in his grasp.

'Charlie got into a fight over his little brother a week or so before he was killed. Matt Hecht called you a coward. There was three of them but Charlie took them on anyway.'

A great swell of emotion arose within him. It threatened to choke him. He could not move, he could not speak but stared as if in a trance at the delicate transparent veins in the sick woman's hand. When it became apparent to the woman that Caleb was not going to respond she pressed on with another matter that was of solemn moment to her.

'Caleb, I'm dying . . . '

His head jerked up and for the first time he looked directly at Elvira. Anticipating his rebuttal of her forthright statement she shook her head to forestall his protestations.

'I want you to promise you'll take care of Gale and little Caleb when I'm gone.'

He could not speak. This request was more than he was capable of. Her words terrified him.

'You hear me Caleb? I need to know before I go.'

'I am not a fit person for such a task,' he managed at last.

'There is no one else, Caleb. You must promise. I must know before I die.'

'Maybe you won't die,' he protested weakly. 'We should get a doctor and find a cure. It's best the children have their mother with them.'

'I'm dying, Caleb. I have resigned myself to that fact and made my peace with the Lord. Promise me now on my deathbed you'll look after my children when I'm gone.' She rallied sufficiently to tighten her grip on his hand. 'Promise me, Caleb . . . '

He could see there would be no rest for her until he promised to do what she asked. 'I promise,' he whispered.

'One more thing, Caleb. Take me back home so I can be with Charlie.'

This seemed a small request after he had been forced make the promise to undertake the much bigger task of becoming nursemaid to two small children.

'I promise.'

10

'Pull the wagon around the rear of the bank,' the leader, big and burly and bearded, instructed.

There were seven of them in the gang — all tough, grim-looking men loaded down with hardware. As instructed Tom Hardy, the driver of the wagon, drove the vehicle down a side alley and pulled up at the rear of the bank.

They were well-versed regarding the geography of the town. Two members of the gang, James Vance and Tom Hardy, had visited Musgrave a few weeks earlier, reported back to the boss and the plans were laid. Now some of the gang were spreading out along the street, dismounting and making pretence of tying up their horses, checking harness and examining the condition of their mounts. It was all perfectly normal behaviour for horsemen after a hard ride. But there was purpose to this idling.

With the information supplied by Vance and Hardy the raid on the bank had been meticulously planned. Once the raid began the men on the street would create a diversion by yelling and firing off their weapons, discouraging any challenge that might be mounted by the townspeople.

The bank was already open and customers were inside making transactions when three armed men burst in through the front doors.

'Everyone on the floor! Down now!'

The commands were yelled and large pistols were brandished to emphasize the threat. As the terrified customers complied two of the armed men strode to the counter and shoved guns into the tellers' faces.

'Fill these!'

Gunnysacks were pushed inside to the frightened bank men.

'Any funny business or trying to raise the alarm and we shoot everyone in sight.'

The terrified clerks grabbed the sacks and began stuffing them with bank-notes.

Meanwhile the third man, James Vance, had closed and bolted the front door. He then ran towards the rear of the bank and kicked open another door leading to offices. There were two clerks sitting at desks. One of the clerks was in the act of pulling a gun from a drawer. Without hesitation the raider fired two shots and the man was knocked back in his chair, his mouth opening and closing as the bullets smashed into him and his life's blood drained away.

'Get that back door opened or you're dead too!' yelled the gunman.

The frightened clerk jumped to his feet and grabbed a bunch of keys from a hook on the wall. His hands trembled so much the keys tumbled to the floor.

'You goddamn clumsy cuss!' As the gunman yelled at the frightened clerk he noticed the iron safe in the corner. 'And get that safe open.'

'Yes sir.'

The clerk bent over the safe, fumbled with the keys and began the process of unlocking the heavy door. Vance watched avidly as it swung open. With a savage blow he smashed the barrel of his pistol into the clerk's skull. The stricken man collapsed without a sound and lay motionless beside the safe he had just opened.

Vance looked inside and gave a low whistle. Quickly he grabbed the keys and ran to the back door. Hardy was waiting outside.

'Hell, Tom, we hit pay dirt. There's a load of gold bullion here. Help me get it loaded.'

Inside the iron safe gold bars were stacked several layers deep.

'Jesus, Vance, this'll set us up for life.'

The two raiders worked frantically, loading the gold ingots into the wagon parked outside the rear of the bank. Before they finished the men who had looted the counter came racing through.

'One of you fellas, hold them people out front!' Vance yelled. 'We got ourselves a fortune in gold here. Help us get it loaded.'

The men were carrying sacks of money that were to be hidden in the wagon. The idea was for the wagon to make a quick departure from the town while the gang created a diversion. They were to meet up at a prearranged rendezvous and divvy up the proceeds of the robbery. That plan was ditched now that the robbers had stumbled across the gold bullion.

One of the raiders ran back into the interior of the bank in time to see a clerk in the act of unbolting the front door. Callously the bank robber shot the man in the back.

'Everyone down on the floor,' he yelled.

The shocked customers and bank tellers immediately obeyed. Seeing a man gunned down knocked any resistance out of them.

Outside in the street the raiders, hearing the shots, quickly mounted up and drew weapons. Overseeing the raid was the big, bearded leader. He rode towards the entrance of the bank as he saw the door opening. Expecting a member of the public or the bank to emerge he was surprised to see one of his own men.

'Parrish, what the hell's going on?' he yelled.

'They found a heap of gold out back. Need a hand loading it.'

The leader waved his support troops forward.

'Follow me!' he bellowed. He urged his horse towards the alleyway that led off the street, the remainder of the gang poured in after him. At the rear of the bank the big man discovered his men busily loading gold bars into the wagon. A grim smile broke across that broad face.

'Jackson, you come back up the street with me. We'll hold off anyone brave enough to interfere. The rest keep loading. Don't leave a grain of that there yalla stuff behind. But hurry.'

He wheeled his big stallion back the way he had come and pulled up just inside the mouth of the alley.

'Fire at anything that moves,' he ordered his companion. 'We gotta give them boys time to get that gold loaded.'

By now men and women were coming out on the boardwalk, looking around them, wondering where the shots had come from and what they heralded. The two riders in the alleyway holstered their pistols and pulled out rifles in their place.

'Let's shoot a few. That'll keep their heads down.'

A man in shirt and braces was standing in front of a building that had a sign advertising O'Brien Surveying Services. He held a pistol in his hand and was gazing across the road at the bank. The bearded leader took aim with his rifle and pulled the trigger. The surveyor staggered back as a crimson stain appeared on his shirtfront. His backward movement was halted as he hit the glass window with the gilt lettering publicizing his services. The glass gave way under the impact.

Accompanied by the sound of breaking glass the surveyor collapsed into the shop, coming to rest with his boots sticking out into the street.

Whooping with excitement the marksmen in the alleyway began firing indiscriminately at anyone within range of their guns. The shooting was having the desired effect and the street cleared except for a wounded man in a suit who was crawling in the dirt towards the shelter of a water barrel, his derby lying in the middle of the road where it had fallen from his head when he had been shot.

'It's like shooting chickens in a henrun,' Len Jackson crowed.

With the street deserted the raiders began to fire at windows and shop signs. It was a terrifying display of firepower as the marksmen emptied magazines into the buildings of Musgrave.

Another of the gang spurred up the alleyway to the two marksmen.

'All loaded back here,' he yelled. 'Time to light out.'

'Get the wagon rolling. We'll meet you at the edge of town.'

There was a further fusillade of shots into the street, then the two marksmen urged their mounts out in the open and began a slow retreat. While one man fired his rifle to discourage pursuit the other rode on. Then he would fire while his companion retreated further. The only response was a few scattered shots from some of the brave townspeople, which came nowhere near hitting the two horsemen.

The gang had successfully looted the bank of Musgrave and were escaping unopposed with their plunder.

11

Tom Hardy yelled and cursed his team of horses as they hauled into the traces to get the heavily laden wagon moving. With a protesting screech from the nearside wheel the wagon lurched into motion.

'Yippee! Easy living, here we come!'

The whip cracked and lashed at the hides of the horses, urging them forward. The bandits had mapped out the course the wagon was to take when fleeing the town, but for Hardy there was one task remaining before he vacated this beleaguered town.

A certain unsavoury bug needed squashing and Hardy was not going to pass up on the chance to do the squashing. He had marked out the shack where Caleb Blood hung out and that was where he was heading. One factor was nagging at his consciousness and that was the noise from the nearside wheel. It signalled trouble and Hardy was hoping the wheel would hold out.

Caleb Blood heard the shooting from his prone position on a bed of warm straw inside the livery. He was feeling pleasantly drowsy and when the shooting started up was content to remain where he was. Not so Marty Sandford, the liveryman.

Marty rushed from his little office, where he had been figuring whether he was making enough money to maybe employ Caleb on a regular basis. As the shots rang out Marty grabbed up his Remington rifle. Caleb heard the liveryman clatter outside but made no move to investigate further. He could hear the firing increasing in intensity.

'Springfields,' he muttered. 'What the hell's going on?'

He searched in the hay for the bottle that had got him off to sleep last night. He sucked at the dregs, then lay back and listened to the gunfire. It was the spark that set up the images in his imagination from which he was perpetually fleeing. He put his hands up as if to ward off the ghosts of the screaming women and children who had suddenly risen from the dead.

'No . . . ' he moaned.

And while the battle in the streets of Musgrave raged another battle was fought in Caleb Blood's memories.

Riders racing up with torches and the flames eating hungrily at the wooden structure of the church. A huge bearded figure loomed up in his imagination. A pistol barked and Caleb felt the pain in his arm. And then his own gun was in his hand and he was squeezing the trigger.

Caleb was thrashing around in the straw, moaning as the terrible images seared his mind. In his imagination he was on his knees in front of the burning church, his hands on fire, trying to blot out the screaming.

★ ★ ★

The wagon loaded with the gold stopped at the dilapidated shack on the outskirts of Musgrave. The rest of the gang crowded around on horses made restless by the gunfire.

'What the hell!' Vance yelled at his partner.

'I've a score to settle,' snarled Tom Hardy.

He jumped from the seat of the wagon and ran to the door of the shack. He did not bother to knock but booted the rickety door to destruction. With his pistol out he charged inside.

'Swamper, I come to kill you!'

To Hardy's chagrin there was no response. He cursed and waved his pistol at the dim interior. Then he noticed a movement from the bed in one corner and fired instinctively. Outside Hardy could hear Vance yelling. Cursing he turned and ran outside again.

'Hardy, for God's sake come on. Get this goddamn wagon moving.'

Hardy vaulted into the seat of the wagon and picked up his whip. 'Gee up!'

His companions were milling round, casting nervous glances back towards the town. By now they could see the two men acting as rearguard coming towards them and turning in the saddle to fire the occasional shot. The wagon lurched forward. Hardy was flailing the horses mercilessly with his whip.

'Giddy up, goddamn lazy critters.'

The faulty wheel squealed in protest, then the inevitable happened. It was the extra weight of the gold bullion that was the deciding factor and the wheel collapsed with the noise of splintering wood. The wagon tipped to one side and jerked to an abrupt halt. Had he not had his feet braced against the footboard Hardy would have pitched over on to the harnessed horses.

'Goddamn blasted bloody wagon . . .'

Hardy lent over and examined the ruined wheel. He raised his eyes and stared aghast at his companions. By then the bearded leader had caught up with his gang.

'What the goddamn hell's going on?'

Like the man himself the voice was huge and resonant.

'We got trouble with the wagon,' Vance yelled. 'Goddamn wheel's come off!'

'Hell, it's the weight of all that gold. There's a wagon by that shack. It'll be quicker to transfer the gold to that. Someone hitch our team up while the rest of you get the goddamn gold loaded. Jackson and myself will keep any interference at bay. Now get going pronto. I don't want this town getting the courage to tackle us all of a sudden.'

At that moment a rifle cracked from the main street. A horse jumped and whinnied as a bullet nicked it.

'Hell's bells, someone's shooting at us.'

Horses were stamping around, panicked by the squeals of the wounded beast. The men assigned to their various tasks dismounted just as another shot winged their way. No one was hit and the raiders quickly tied up the nervous horses to the stalled wagon.

Carrying his rifle Len Jackson ran to the lee of a nearby building. More shots were being fired towards the bandits. A bullet hit the wagon as the men were unloading the gold and transferring it to the new vehicle. Men were cussing and working and casting anxious looks in the direction from which the shots were coming.

'Can you see him?' roared the leader. He had stayed mounted but had guided his big stallion behind the stalled wagon.

'There,' yelled Jackson, a thin beanpole of a man with a stovepipe hat. 'Just this side of the livery.'

'I see him. He pokes his head out, fires, then dodges back in again. Wait for his next shot and we both blast that corner to kingdom come.'

Jackson crouched with his rifle aimed at the sniper's position. A head appeared and the marksman took aim at the men working at the wagons. Before he could let loose Len Jackson and his boss fired together, aiming several shots at the sniper. Wood chips flew from the corner of the building. The bandits saw the rifle dip and slide to one side but kept up their fire. A figure staggered back from the corner and they poured shot after shot into him. The wounded man was punched back as bullets peppered his torso and he collapsed on his back.

'Whoopee, got the goddamn bastard.'

'Just keep shooting. Make them keep their heads down.'

With so many hands work was progressing well and the gold was soon transferred to the new wagon. Tom Hardy climbed aboard and set the team moving. The wagon rolled out on the road and he whipped the team to faster efforts.

'Come on. Let's get outta here.'

The raiders rode after the wagon, firing a few parting shots as they went. In a very short time nothing could be seen of the bandits but the dust they had kicked up as they fled the town leaving behind a shocked populace and several dead bodies.

12

An eerie silence settled over Musgrave as the citizens crept cautiously from their homes and places of business to survey the destruction wreaked on their town by the raiders.

'Timmy!' a portly woman cried as she rushed to the man propped up against the water butt. 'Help me, someone.'

There was plenty of help as men came forward to carry the wounded man to the doctor's office. Alerted by the shooting the doctor arrived on the scene.

'Good God, what happened?'

'Bank raid, Doc. Bandits shot up the town and cleaned out the bank.'

'How many more wounded?'

'Ain't sure.'

Doctor Coates directed the men carrying the wounded Timmy into his surgery. The portly woman was Timmy's wife. She stayed by the injured man's side, moaning his name over and over again.

'Leave him with me. Go back into town and bring back anyone else needs attention,' the doctor ordered the volunteers as he took off his coat and rolled up his sleeves.

The small group of helpers walked back to the main street where all the shooting had taken place. They found that the body of the surveyor Jonah O'Brien had been retrieved from the ruins of his front window and laid out on the boardwalk. A thoughtful soul had brought a blanket and covered up the remains. A dishevelled Caleb Blood stood blinking in the sunlight at the entrance of the livery stables.

'What's going on?' he called.

'Bank's been robbed. Shot Timmy Joyce. He's at the doc's getting patched up. O'Brien the surveyor's dead.'

The onlookers watched as another body was carried from an alleyway.

'Who is it?'

'Marty Sandford. Caught a chest full of lead.'

'Marty . . . '

Caleb took a step forward. There was no need to ask if the liveryman was dead. His shirtfront was matted in dark blood.

'Not Marty . . . hell, not Marty . . . '

They carried the dead man to the survey office and laid him on the boardwalk alongside O'Brien. The blanket was rearranged to cover both heads but the ruined chest of Marty offended one man. He went inside O'Brien's office and returned shortly with a coat that must have belonged to the surveyor. He used the coat to cover O'Brien and rearranged the blanket over Marty.

Caleb came and knelt beside the bodies. Another man came up and displayed the rifle Marty had used to such good effect against the raiders.

'This is Marty's gun. What'll I do with it?'

'Put it inside the livery,' Caleb said, not looking up. 'Oh, Marty, why did you do it? You goddamn brave old fool.'

There was a sudden wailing and Doc Coates came onto the street with an arm around Mrs Joyce. The watchers waited in silence. Doctor Coates looked up and shook his head.

'Damn them bloody bandits to hell and back!' someone growled. 'Killing decent people just like that. It ain't right.'

More and more people were coming into the street now that the danger had passed. Caleb stayed kneeling by the dead Marty, holding the hand of the liveryman. His head was bowed and he appeared deeply moved by the death of his friend, though it was hard to tell, for his long untamed hair hung down and obscured his face.

A large man dressed in a business suit approached the crowd gathered outside the surveyor's office. People made way for him. His bald head and face were shiny with sweat and he wiped at himself with a handkerchief. It was Percy Starr, the bank manager.

'Dear God, this is the worst day of my life,' he burst out. 'They cleared out the bank.' Then he saw the bodies. 'Oh my, this is terrible . . . who . . . who is that?'

'Jonah O'Brien and Marty Sandford. They got Timmy Joyce as well. The doc's just taken his wife . . . widow home.'

'We got to send a message to the sheriff at Newtown. Tell him what's happened. They need to get a posse together and find the bandits.'

'The hell, we can't wait for Newtown,' a voice broke in. 'They'll be long gone afore Newtown gets on the case. We got enough men here to form a posse. I say let's saddle up and get after those varmints.'

People were turning to the speaker. Jess Jordan was standing feet astride and glaring angrily around at the crowd.

'Hell, he's right. They rode out only a

short while ago. If we hurry we can catch up with them outlaws. Give them a taste of their own medicine.'

By now the crowd were stirred up and angry voices were being raised.

'Yeah, let's do it. We got enough men and guns here to ride them varmints down.'

The decision was unanimous and men were hurrying purposefully for horses and weapons. It took a while but a sizeable body of men assembled in the street, all armed and mounted. Jess Jordan the saloonkeeper took charge.

'Let's get this wrapped up,' he yelled from atop his mount. 'When we bring them murdering bastards back there's drinks on the house all night for every man riding in this posse.'

There was a ragged cheer and the posse set out, spurring down the main street, kicking up clouds of dust and heading in the direction the bank robbers had taken. The men were keyed up and excited, confident of their success in the pursuit of the bandits.

Caleb Blood did not join the posse. As the townsmen rode out he rose from his vigil by the liveryman and stood undecided as to his next move.

'Caleb,' a voice called.

He turned and saw Crystal across the street. When the trouble started she had been in the Horn of Plenty and had stayed there. Now she was heading back to her cabin.

'Walk back home with me, Caleb. The children most likely will be frightened by all this upset.'

He nodded and walked across to her. She linked arms with him.

'Did I hear right that Marty was killed?' she asked.

He nodded. 'The old fool went after the raiders. Took them on single-handed.'

There was a catch in Caleb's voice as he spoke. Sensing his distress Crystal squeezed his arm.

'I'm sorry, Caleb. He was such a sweet old man. You and he were friends.'

'Aye.'

They walked in silence after that and it was only as they approached the shack that Crystal spoke again.

'There's a wagon parked outside. Not more of your family come to stay?' she quipped.

'I don't think so. It's got a broken wheel. Whoever it was must have abandoned it.'

It was only as they got closer that they realized Elvira's wagon was no longer parked by the cabin.

'Musta borrowed our wagon. I hope they didn't upset the children.'

'Naw, they'll be inside with their ma now.'

But the children weren't in the cabin. There was an ominous silence within as the two adults entered. Crystal slung her bag on the table and moved to the bed in the corner.

'Elvira,' she called softly.

There was no answer. She bent over the bed, then she started back, her hand to her mouth.

'Oh my God!'

It was a cry laced with despair and horror.

13

Crystal was clinging to Caleb, her head pressed against his chest. As he held her and felt her tremors he was thinking she reminded him of a frightened puppy he had rescued once, whose mother a wolf had killed. Suddenly she pulled back and looked up at him, beginning to push away from his comforting embrace.

'The children, Caleb . . . what about Gale and little Caleb?'

He blinked and stared at her. 'They're probably hiding out back somewhere. I'll go outside and call them.'

Crystal could not quell the feeling of dread rising up in her. 'Oh Caleb, please don't let anything happen to them.'

'You're sure Elvira's dead?' he asked. He had not yet been able to go over to the bed in the corner.

'Oh Caleb, it's terrible. Who could do such a thing — to shoot a poor sick woman?'

He wanted a drink, wanted to pour the nectar of oblivion into him and blot out the horrors that were crowding in on him. First Marty lying out in the street with his chest torn to ribbons with rifle bullets, then the discovery of Elvira shot in her bed. He needed a drink and then he would have the courage to go out and look for the children. But Crystal was pushing him towards the door. In the end he had to go outside with Crystal to search for the children.

'Gale, Caleb!' Crystal called.

She was walking around the side of the shack, looking over at the weeds growing tall in the wasteland that backed up on to their little home. Caleb went to the wagon with the broken wheel and studied the scuffed earth.

As he pored over the evidence printed in the dirt he began to piece together what had happened here. He made bigger and wider circles around the wagon and the cabin, noting the places where someone had knelt in the lee of a shack and the litter of spent shells that indicated a rifleman firing into the town.

Between the space occupied by the missing wagon and the broken one there were deep imprints of men engaged in the task of transferring cargo. Slowly he pieced together the story etched into the dirt. As he worked he could hear Crystal calling the children. Her shouts were becoming louder and more desperate.

'Gale, Caleb, where are you, honey?'

She came up to him as he stood peering at the churned-up ground. He looked up and saw the fear in her eyes.

'Why don't they come, Caleb?'

A dread was growing in his mind. Their mother shot to death in her bed and the children missing.

'Maybe they ran into town to get help,' he suggested, trying to reassure himself as much as Crystal.

'They were fearful the men who drove them from their home would come after them. I told them the wagon was a safe refuge. If they hid inside then no harm would come to them. Oh, Caleb, you don't think they've been taken?'

When she told him the wagon was their safe refuge he knew with certainty what had happened.

'I need a drink.'

She stepped back from him. He could not look her in the eye but turned and started for the cabin.

'Is that what's important, Caleb?'

She could not help herself. Her resentment and fear burst like a dam, poured out and washed over him. It was dread for the children that forced her to say the things she did.

'Your sister is shot dead while lying helpless in her bed. Her children are missing and all you want to do is fill your belly with whiskey.'

It was all there in her voice, his neglect, the constant craving for alcohol, the indifference to everything other than his needs rather than her own desires. But that was as nothing compared to the nameless fear that tore at her insides, her dread for children who had wormed their way into her heart. It was this fear that made her reckless and drove her to lash him with her tongue.

'What are you, Caleb Blood? What sort of man are you? I . . . I thought I saw something in you that was redeemable. I tried to help you by taking you in and even supplied you with whiskey to help you hide from your demons. But I know now that was a mistake. How long must you go on hiding? For the rest of your life? Well go on, Caleb Blood. Drink yourself to death. I'll go find someone who can help me find those poor kids. Certainly you're a pitiable excuse for an uncle — a feeble excuse for a man!'

He did not turn around but moved to the cabin door and went inside where he stood motionless, not seeing anything, lost in some private world of pain and guilt. From outside came the sound of weeping. Slowly he walked across to the bed and looked down at the horror that had been Elvira.

A bullet had entered just beneath her nose and tore her upper lip apart. Vestiges of shattered teeth were exposed as shining white fragments amongst the blood and torn flesh. Slowly he dropped to his knees beside the cot.

'Elvira,' he whispered, 'I'm sorry.'

Behind him he heard the door open as Crystal came inside.

'Caleb.' Her voice was soft and low, full of contrition. 'I did not mean to hurt you. Please forgive me.'

He made no response but stayed by the bed with his head bowed. He could hear the rustle of her movements as she went about some task. There was the distinct sound of a cork popping from a bottle and the gush of liquid as a glass was filled. She came and stood beside him.

'Here.'

The tantalizing aroma of bourbon

was strong in his nostrils. His body was crying out for the solace the drink bestowed upon him. All his senses craved for the blessing of the alcohol-laced blunting of painful memories and the accompanying guilt.

'I'm sorry, Caleb. Won't you please forgive me.'

'One day she bade me come and sit by her side. She told me she was dying and when I tried to reassure her she hushed me up. Elvira knew she was dying and yet her concern was not for herself. She made me promise to take care of Caleb and Gale. And I made that promise.'

He reached out and tugged the blanket up over the ruined face. For a moment he stayed where he was, then got to his feet and stood staring down at the bed. After many moments he turned and looked at Crystal. She stood watching him, her face puffy from weeping, a scared look in her eyes. He ignored the glass of bourbon she was holding.

'I believe those raiders stole our children. I do not know what they had against Elvira to shoot her like that. Perhaps they were paid by the people back in Newtown to kill her so they could take over Charlie's ranch. That's why they were driven out. Someone wants that ranch. Elvira and her children stood in the way of them getting it.' He took the glass from her hand walked past her to the table and set it down. 'When I bring back the children I have to take Elvira home. That was a promise I also made to her.'

14

The livery stable was empty when Caleb went back down. Just inside the door was the rifle Marty had been using to shoot at the raiders. Caleb picked it up and went into Marty's office. After rooting around he found the Colt in a drawer. On a shelf were stacked a couple of boxes of shells and he took these as well. There were small sacks of hay and oats which Marty stocked and sold to customers wanting to carry fuel for their mounts. Caleb piled as many as he could carry in his arms before going back up to the shack. Crystal was standing outside watching out for him.

'What are you doing, Caleb?'

'If you want to help go down to the meadow and bring the horses back here.'

The horses that had pulled the wagon and brought Elvira and her children to Musgrave had been left to graze in the free range at the edge of town. They had been hobbled to keep them from wandering too far. Crystal looked at him doubtfully but said nothing and went to find the horses.

Caleb laid down the weapons and the forage by the front door of the shack and went inside. He spent a few moments putting together supplies for the journey he was planning.

The glass of whiskey Crystal had poured for him as a peace offering was still on the table along with the bottle. For long agonizing moments he stood by the table trying not to look at the bottle and glass. The strong aroma of the liquor awakened his compulsion for the alcohol. He reached out a hand towards the tempting liquor. Just short of the glass he stopped and held his hand there, his eyes wide with longing. As he stood like this his hand outstretched he noticed for the first time the tremor. His hand trembled like a man with the ague.

'I need this. I need it now.' He grabbed the glass, raised it and held it under his nose and inhaled. 'Aaahh . . . I do need this . . . '

As he began to tip the glass towards his lips there came a slight noise from the direction of the bed. He started and some of the liquor spilled on his hand. Slowly his head turned and he stared with some apprehension at the covered-up figure in the bed. The shape of his dead sister-in-law was discernible beneath the covers. He stood there for long agonizing moments, staring hard.

'Elvira . . . '

There was no response. His hand was still trembling and his breath was coming more quickly as he set the glass back on the table without drinking. He had to put both hands flat on the table and support himself for several moments before he could continue.

It was with a feeling of relief he stepped outside with his packet of food and placed it with the stuff he had foraged from the livery. Then he began a comprehensive study of the area around the shack and the abandoned wagon. At times he hunkered down and examined in detail some of the prints.

Next he turned his attention to the wagon, walking around it and noting any markings on the bodywork. He climbed up to the driving seat and spent some time looking inside the toolbox before clambering inside the body of the wagon. When Crystal arrived back with the horses he was sitting on the door stoop, gazing off into the distance.

'What is it, Caleb. Are you really going after those killers?'

'If I don't make it back can you at least have Elvira's remains sent back to Newtown to be buried with Charlie?'

Suddenly her arms were clamped around his neck.

'It's my fault, isn't it, Caleb? If I hadn't told the children to go in the wagon they'd be safe with us.'

'We don't know that. All we know is that those raiders came by, shot Elvira and the children are missing. Why this family should be targeted is a mystery. As I said, the killers might have been employed by the people back in Newtown who drove them out.'

'Let me go with you, Caleb.'

He shook his head. 'I need you to take care of things here. What if the kids come back of their own accord and find their ma with a hole in her face? They'll need you, Crystal. They'll need you more than they need me. You've been more an aunt to them than I've ever been an uncle.'

He had to use a little force to remove her hands from around his neck before turning his attention to the horses.

There was no saddle and he had to fashion a bridle from the wagon harness. He threw a blanket over the pinto with the intention of riding Indian style. As he tied his supplies to the second horse he thought he recognized the beast.

'If I remember right you must be Caesar. Charlie set a lotta store by you. Maybe we'll come through this, old-timer, and maybe not.' Caleb climbed aboard his mount. ''Bye, Crystal. Remember what I said about sending Elvira back home.' He kicked his heels in the horse's flanks. 'Gee up there.'

Crystal stood with her arms wrapped around her and watched Caleb ride away till she could no longer see him.

'Come back to me, Caleb,' she murmured. 'I know I ain't much to come back to but you're everything to me.'

She stood by the door of the shack, reluctant to go inside. It distressed her that the grisly remains of Elvira were all that awaited her. For a short time the children of the dead woman had been hers to care for; her maternal instincts had been aroused and she had been almost happy with them. In turn the children had trusted her. She had told them they would be safe in the wagon but now they were gone and she dared not speculate on their fate.

She leaned her head against the door and the tears she had not shed since childhood flowed down her cheeks.

15

It was getting towards dusk when Caleb heard the horsemen somewhere up ahead. He turned his mount off the trail, moved back into the chaparral and dismounted. He had no holster so the Colt was pushed inside his waistband; briefly he touched the bone handle as if to reassure himself it was still there. The rifle was lashed to the packhorse and he eased it from the straps that held it secure.

The animals, suitably rested and fed on the free grazing, had stood up well to the ride. He had not pushed them, content to make progress steadily. Now they stood patiently as he waited for the horsemen to come into view.

From the reverberation of the earth Caleb reckoned a sizable body of horsemen were coming his way. He wished he had better cover and instinctively moved further back from the trail. The dust was rising now as they came on and he watched it, judging the distance of the riders from his position.

The thunder of the many hoofs made the earth tremble as they came into view. He narrowed his eyes, squinting into the day's dullness that heralded the advent of nightfall. His hands tightened on the rifle as he watched. Then he relaxed as he identified the riders now heading back the way he had just come.

Jess Jordan headed the pack. No one in the posse glanced to either side as they rode past. Caleb made no move to attract attention but stood motionless in the cover of the chaparral. The posse swept on down the trail towards Musgrave and was almost out of sight before Caleb stirred.

Thoughtfully he replaced the rifle back in the makeshift holding straps. There had been no obvious signs of prisoners amongst the riders, nor did any of the mounts carry what might have been the booty that had been stolen from the bank by the bandits. He led his mounts back on to the trail and continued his journey.

Before the night fell completely into darkness Caleb rode off the trail a goodly pace before he picked a site for camp. He hobbled his mounts and scoured around for firewood. Within a short time he had a blazing campfire with the coffee pot bubbling over the flames. As he poured the coffee he could not control the way his enamel mug and the pot rattled together.

He prepared no food, for he was not hungry. When he wrapped himself in his blankets the shaking had spread throughout his body. His teeth chattered together and he could see streaks of light inside his eyelids when he closed them. As the night progressed the memories came thick and fast to haunt him. Again and again the burning church materialized in his dreams.

'*I tried to save you,*' he called out and

held his blistered hands up as witness of his failure.

The screams from amidst the flames grew more persistent and shrill.

'*It wasn't my fault! I tried! God knows I tried!*'

When morning dawned he was more exhausted than when he had lain down. He got his fire rekindled and spilled coffee as his trembling increased. His mug clattered against his teeth when he tried to drink.

When he began his journey again he leaned forward on his horse's neck and was not sure what direction he was supposed to be heading. He allowed the horses to take over and clung to the back of his mount while horrors blossomed in his mind and became real perils he had to overcome. Sometimes he passed out and clung to his mount purely by instinct. The horses plodded on placidly, seemingly not bothered by the strange behaviour of their new master.

He was not sure how long he was in

this state of dementia. The horses had stopped and he surfaced from a deep and disturbing nightmare. Slowly he opened his eyes then closed them again as if the sunlight was too much. He stayed clinging to the back of his mount, wondering where he was.

'Howdy fella, you all right?'

Slowly he forced his eyes open again. A bearded face was peering curiously at him, the head canted to one side.

'Uh-uh.' Cautiously he raised his head. The world stayed stable enough for him to sit up. 'Where am I?' he croaked.

'Benjamin Crossing.'

He had landed amidst a cluster of wooden shacks.

'You look as if you need a drink, young 'un.'

Caleb shook his head, then noticed the water trough. His thirsty mounts were busy drinking, their nozzles buried deep in the water.

Slowly he slid from the pinto, his body aching from the unaccustomed riding. Without a word to the curious watcher he followed his mounts' example and buried his head in the water.

'Hey fella, that's for animals, that water is. No one in their sensible mind would drink water from a horse trough.'

Caleb raised his head, gargled and spat water into the dust.

'Tastes good to me.'

He fumbled in his shirt pocket and pulled out a crumpled piece of paper. He held it out to the bearded man.

'I'm looking for this place.'

He had found the receipt inside the wagon abandoned by the bandits. The man he showed the paper to squinted at the print.

'Wilkinson's General Supplies. Why hell, that's right here. Wannetta Wilkinson runs this place. Her husband was the proprietor but he up and died. Wannetta's a widow now.'

'Where can I find this Wannetta?'

The bearded gent pointed to a large building with a faded sign tacked to the front. Wilkinson's General Supplies was printed on the warped board.

'Inside there. Mind, she don't give no credit,' his informant said eyeing up the dishevelled state of the newcomer with his unshorn hair and unkempt appearance.

Caleb started forward, stumbled slightly, recovered and walked on.

It was dim inside the store, for which Caleb was thankful. The bright sun had been hurtful to his eyes. The room he entered was spacious with tables and chairs crowded into one corner. A rough bar had been constructed of old molasses barrels as the base and with boards nailed in place. The rest of the room was taken up with barrels, sacks and boxes of dry goods. Someone in denims and a plaid shirt was filling bottles from a keg.

'Howdy fella, what's your poison? First one's on the house, then fifty cents a bottle of this here rotgut. Guaranteed to make you forget all your woes and damage beyond repair the lining of your stomach.'

The smell of raw spirits was strong in the room. Caleb stood just inside the door and swayed slightly as the old desires took over. He wanted nothing more than to go to the bar and fill his belly with the mind-numbing ambrosia. Instead he walked up to the counter and held out the bill he had found inside the bandits' abandoned wagon.

'I'm trying to find the fella as bought these goods.'

It was only when he was close he could see the person he addressed was a female. She had leathery skin and short grey hair and she never took her attention from her task of decanting the liquor. The smell was intense in his nostrils and he stared hard at the woman, willing her to look at him.

'Can't tell you nothing, son. I have a hundred traders a week come through here, then roll on through like tumbleweed leaving not a trace of their passing.'

Caleb laid the bill on the counter and put both hands flat either side of it and leaned forward.

'Can't or won't?'

'I run a business here, son, not an information bureau. Now, you wanna buy something, then buy it, otherwise don't be wasting my time. I'm a busy woman.'

He breathed deep and hard trying to hold down his anger and frustration.

'The men I'm looking for abducted a little girl and her brother. I fear for their safety. I just want them back.'

For the first time she turned her gaze on him, looked him over before commenting: 'You don't look the sorta fella would be bothered with children.'

'I'm their uncle.'

'Why'd they snatch them?'

Caleb shrugged. 'You might as well ask, why's a wolf snatch a calf? These fellas shot their mother and made off with the children. I just know I gotta get them back afore something terrible happens to them.'

Her eyes were pale blue and faded. She stared at him a long time. He let her stare, waiting. At last she reached out, pulled the bill towards her, studied it.

16

The opening into the hills was well hidden. Tall trees aided by a fold in the facing stack fooled the eye and indicated only an impenetrable mass of cliff-like hillocks. Caleb guided his mount through the tangle of undergrowth till he found the hidden stream.

'So far so good,' he muttered.

He let the animals drink at the clear running water, then urged the pinto forward. The handle of a shovel poked up from his pack and along with a pickaxe was amongst some of the items he had purchased from Wannetta Wilkinson.

'You gotta have an excuse for going into Death Gulch,' the old woman had advised. 'Hunting gold is a wasteful pastime.'

She had rummaged in a drawer and come up with a much-creased piece of parchment on which were traced the faint outlines of a map. It was indistinct, the faded lettering all but legible.

'Took this from a fella as died here on me. Afore he died he tried to sell the map to me. Said as a fella back in Kansas City sold it to him. Shows the location of a goldmine. Might be useful to show as to why you is poking around in them thar hills.' Her shrewd old eyes were inscrutable as she added, 'Mind you, if you find any gold I want twenty per cent.'

When he smelled the wood smoke he tethered the animals and went forward on foot. A cabin had been built bordering the stream he had been following. The wagon that had been parked outside Crystal's shack stood nearby. Three men were sitting around a cook fire in front of the cabin. As he watched he saw a bottle being passed around. One of the men was a huge bearded fellow and Caleb spent some time studying him. There was something familiar about the big man.

'How the hell they get that wagon in there?' he muttered before gliding back to his mounts.

He took a roundabout route, casting for the trail that would be negotiable by vehicle. When he eventually found what he was seeking he sat atop his mount for a while deep in thought. He yawned widely and felt again the need for a drink pulling at him. Wearily he shook himself awake, made his preparations, then proceeded down the wagon trail till he came in sight of the cabin.

As was the custom when coming on an isolated camp he yelled out a greeting. He prodded the pinto forward and rode on towards the cabin. What he saw there made him pull up abruptly and throw his hands in the air. Three guns were un-leathered and pointing steadily at him.

'Hell, fellas, I ain't looking for no trouble.'

He sat atop his pinto with his lank unruly hair and stubbly cheeks looking just like a thousand other saddle bums. The gunmen stared, flinty-eyed, and Caleb could feel the tension coming off them.

'What you doing here, stranger?'

'Ain't doing nothing in particular. Just riding through and smelled the fire. Thought I might catch some hot coffee.'

'Nobody just rides through here. It's private property. We don't never get no travellers this trail.'

'Private! Hell, I ain't seen no signs. Can I put my hands down? It's a mite tiring.'

'Get down off that horse real careful. Parker, see if he's armed.'

Caleb dismounted, keeping his hands in plain sight. A thickset blond man came forward and roughly searched Caleb.

'I ain't got no weapons,' Caleb said helpfully. 'Only a rifle as I use for hunting.'

'Get the rifle, Parker.'

It was the big bearded man who was

giving the orders. Parker searched the packhorse, found the rifle and tossed it over near the fire.

'Now, mister, you tell us what the hell you doing here?'

Caleb shrugged and put his hands out, palms up. 'I tell you, just riding through.'

There was a nod from the big man and Parker stepped in close and coshed Caleb with his revolver. Caleb went down under the blow.

'Aw, why the hell you do that!' he groaned. 'Why you fellas so tetchy?'

The big bearded man was standing over Caleb now, his feet planted astride, his pistol pointed at the man on the ground.

'Tell us why you're here!' he roared. 'Afore I put a bullet in your goddamn head.'

'It's the gold,' Caleb moaned. 'I'm looking for the gold.'

There was a stunned silence from the outlaws, then the big man booted Caleb.

'You son of a bitch, who told you about the gold?'

'Oh, God help me,' Caleb moaned. 'You've found it, haven't you? I'm too late.'

'Shoot the sonabitch,' Parker growled.

'No, wait. If this bum found us maybe others might. We gotta make him talk.' Again the big man kicked Caleb. 'Who told you about the gold?'

Caleb yelped. 'I bought a map but I got lost. The map didn't make no sense.'

'What the hell you talking about — a map?'

'The map showing the gold ... I bought it in good faith, mister.' An edge of cunning crept into Caleb's voice. 'Have you registered the claim yet?'

The outlaws were glancing from one to the other, then at the packhorse with the digging tools plainly visible.

'You mean you came up here looking for gold ... prospecting like?'

The outlaws were relaxing as understanding dawned.

'Look, mister, I ain't no claim

jumper. I can help you. I have experience in panning gold.'

'You saying you bought a map and it led you up here to us?' Parker asked, still sceptical. 'Show us this goddamn map.'

Weapons were being lowered along with the bandits' suspicions. Caleb was climbing unsteadily to his feet, rubbing at his head.

'Why the hell you hit me so hard, fella?' He swayed slightly, still massaging the lump on his head.

'Just show us the goddamn map, shithead, afore I hit you again!'

Caleb was fumbling amongst the tools. He pulled the shovel from the pack, then the pick. He had his back to the bandits. When he turned he had the map in his hand. The map was draped over Marty's Colt, hiding it from sight.

'I paid twenty-five dollars for this here map.'

With his next action he ruined all hope of deciphering the map for he squeezed the trigger on the Colt. The bullet went through the parchment and the muzzle flash set it on fire.

The bullet hit the big bearded man in the chest. He staggered back and snagged his boot on Caleb's rifle lying where Parker had tossed it. The stricken man went over backwards and flopped into the fire where he thrashed about in the flames, roaring hoarsely.

Ignoring the injured man, Caleb chose Parker as his next target, but the bandit was bringing up his own pistol. The men fired simultaneously, Parker in his hurry triggering too soon. The bullet whistled somewhere over Caleb's shoulder. Caleb's shot was more controlled. They were only yards apart and he could not miss. The bullet hit Parker in the face and the bandit was screaming as he fell back still triggering his pistol, the bullets spraying into the dirt.

The third outlaw, who had holstered his weapon when he sensed there was no danger from the saddle bum, was fast bringing his weapon up. Caleb fired two shots rapidly at the man's torso and the gunman staggered back, his legs crumbled, and suddenly Caleb was left standing alone.

With his own gun empty he quickly strode to the last man he had shot and grabbed up the outlaw's fallen pistol. Crouching down by the dead bandit he scanned the area around the clearing.

Parker lay unmoving. The man whose gun he now had in his hand was still breathing but unconscious. Caleb could hear the breath bubbling in the man's throat. The big bearded man who had fallen on to the fire had rolled to safety and had managed to beat the flames out where his clothes had caught fire.

'Help me,' he moaned hoarsely. His chest was covered with blood from the bullet wound. Caleb slowly walked around the fire. The faggots had been scattered but were still smoking. He stood looking down at the wounded man. Smoke was rising from his smouldering garments.

'Please help me.'

The wounded man held out his blistered and blackened hands in a plea for help. Even his beard had caught some of the fire and his face was charred and blistered also.

'What did you do with the children?'

'Goddamn help me! Can't you see I'm hurt. I got burned in the fire when you shot me, you goddamn son of a bitch!'

For a moment Caleb regarded the suffering man.

'Not so badly burned as the people of Perryville, Major Wesley Harwinton.'

He could see the frown forming on the big man's face.

'Perryville . . . what the hell you talking about?'

'A burning church . . . women and children burned to death . . . '

'Why you saying that? Who are you?'

'Caleb Blood.'

'You! You sonabitch, you shot me at Perryville. But why . . . what were those people to you?'

'Just people. But I don't expect you

to understand that. Now where's the children?'

'Listen, Blood, I have gold. Help me and I'll give you a share.'

Caleb shook his head in disgust, then turned his back on the man and walked towards the wagon. He found the bars of gold stacked inside covered with gunnysacks but no sign of Gale and Caleb.

Next he turned his attention to the cabin. He went to the door and pushed it open. The hinges creaked eerily and he stepped inside, scanning the room. Other than a decrepit stove and a few sticks of ramshackle furniture the place seemed empty.

'Anyone here,' he called and listened. Except for the moaning of Harwinton from outside the place was quiet as a grave. He was about to turn around and leave when on a notion he called out the names of the children. 'Caleb, Gale, are you there?'

There was the faintest of noises from behind a door at the back of the room.

A wooden bar held the door secure. He brought up the gun he had plucked from the wounded bandit, walked across the room to the door, withdrew the bar and pulled it open. Two frightened little faces peered out at him.

17

The first thing James Vance noticed when he came in sight of the cabin was the absence of the wagon. He reined up, a bad feeling starting in his gut. Tom Hardy reined alongside him.

'Well, we're back, Vance.'

'The wagon, Tom, where the hell is the wagon?'

Hardy stared down at the empty space where they had parked the wagon laden with the stolen gold.

'What the . . . ' He urged his horse forward.

'Wait!' Vance called urgently. He had drawn his Colt. 'Let's go down in there real easy. This doesn't look good.'

Two more riders came up behind. One had a dense black beard, a hook nose and deep-set eyes. His companion was a lean youngster with clear-cut tanned face.

'What's up, Vance?'

'Something's up, the wagon's gone.'

'The hell you say.'

'You and Broody stay here,' Vance ordered. 'Tom and me'll ride down and take a look around. Any trouble and you two come in shooting.'

They walked the horses the rest of the way, guns at the ready. Nothing stirred. The camp appeared deserted. Then they saw the blanketed figure lying near the scattered fire and two bodies sprawled nearby. Slowly Vance dismounted. Hardy stayed mounted, his eyes ever watchful, scanning the cabin and surrounds for sign of danger. Vance knelt beside the man wrapped in the blanket. He saw the blackened blistered face and the singed hair.

'Major.'

The eyes in the charred face opened. 'Vance . . . ' The voice was weak.

'What happened?'

'He fooled us . . . thought he was just a saddle bum . . . '

'Who was it, Major?'

'Blood . . . ' The eyes had closed again. 'I'm dying, Vance. Get me a sawbones.'

'Yeah, yeah! Who did it? Who took the gold?'

There was no answer. Vance grabbed Harwinton by his collar and pulled him up.

'Who took the gold!' he yelled.

'Blood . . . Caleb Blood . . . '

By now Hardy had stepped down and was listening to the interrogation.

'Blood! What the hell's he talking about? That swamper fella in the Horn of Plenty was Blood. It can't have been him. He was just a drunken bum.'

Vance shook Harwinton more vigorously. 'What did he look like, this Caleb Blood?' he yelled.

'I . . . didn't recognize him . . . I thought . . . I thought he was just a saddle tramp.'

Vance looked up at his companion. 'You think it was the same fella?'

'It figgers.' Hardy's eyes widened. 'The kids, he came after those brats.'

Hardy turned, strode inside the cabin, then reappeared in the doorway. 'They're gone! It's gotta be him. You shoulda let me kill him that night in Musgrave.'

Vance turned his attention back to Harwinton. 'When did this happen? How long's he been gone . . . how long?'

'Caleb Blood . . . sonabitch . . . sonabitch . . . ' Harwinton was rambling, muttering prayers, his voice getting weaker and weaker.

In disgust Vance released his grip on the man's collar and Harwinton's head fell back.

'We gotta get that wagon back.' He turned and waved at the two men waiting down the trail. 'It shouldn't be too hard to follow. If he tracked it here we can track him.'

★　★　★

Caleb drew rein in front of Wilkinson's General Supplies. When he stepped down from the wagon his legs almost gave way. He leaned against the side of the wagon while his world tilted. When things stabilized somewhat he stepped inside. Wanetta Wilkinson was not in sight but came through from the rear when she heard the door.

'Doggone my hide, if it ain't the gold prospector.'

'I got something for you.'

She was eyeing him up shrewdly. 'Oh, yeah!'

'It's outside in the wagon.'

He turned and went back through the door and she followed. Opening up the tailgate he waited for her to catch up with him.

'Children, what the hell am I to do with children?' she exclaimed peering inside.

'No, not children, something much more precious.' He pulled aside a sack and she gasped when she saw the ingots. 'I guess I owe you one of these for your help, Mrs Wilkinson.'

'Hell's bells . . . ' her eyes widened. 'This the gold from the bank robbery?'

She looked at the horses tied to the wagon. Caleb had taken the outlaws' mounts with him, reluctant to leave them to starve. He followed her gaze.

'The fellas as owned these mounts won't be needing them no more.'

'The bank won't be coming after me looking for this here gold bar?' she asked.

He shook his head. 'Not unless you tell them. But I'd melt it down pronto. It has a stamp on as will identify it.'

The old woman reached out and took hold of an ingot, and gasped as she pulled it out.

'Damn me if 'n this ain't heavy then I'm a Dutchman.' She moved back. 'Thank you, sonny. You gonna disappear with all that there loot?'

'No ma'am, I aim to take it back. It ain't mine but I thought it only right and proper to pay you for your help in recovering it.'

He climbed back on the wagon. 'You take care now, Mrs Wilkinson. Gee up there.'

The old woman stood on the step and watched the wagon drive out of the yard.

'Well I'll be ... ' she muttered. 'Who'd imagined ... '

* * *

Caleb saw that the broken-down wagon had been removed from in front of the shack.

'Crystal!'

There was no reply so he called again. Still no response. His eyes were burning in his head. He'd had no rest for twenty-four hours, driving through the night to put as much distance as possible between himself and the outlaw hideaway. He glanced over his shoulder at the two slight forms inside the wagon. Wrapped in blankets they were fast asleep; like him, they were exhausted by the events of the past few days.

His next stop was the bank. He fell out of the wagon on to the boardwalk, clambered to his feet again and went inside. A few customers were at the counter. Bypassing them Caleb leaned his head against the panel that separated customer from teller.

'I need to see Starr.' It was an effort to keep his eyes open.

'Please take your place in the queue.'

For a moment there was silence as everyone waited to see this filthy creature put in his place. Caleb pulled his pistol and pushed the barrel through one of the little spaces in the panel.

'If Starr ain't out here pronto this bank will be advertising a vacancy.'

There were gasps from behind him and people fell back from the counter.

'I . . . I . . . yes sir . . . straight away, sir.'

The frightened teller scuttled away to an inner office. Caleb put his gun away and wondered whether he would fall down again when he moved from the support of the counter.

The large imperious figure of Percy

Starr appeared. He had dispatched the clerk to fetch Sheriff Julius LeMoyne come over from Newtown to investigate the bank robbery. So far LeMoyne had done nothing, only stay at the Pirouette Hotel and eat and drink at the town's expense.

'What can I do for you?' He peered closer. 'Caleb Blood, isn't it?'

Caleb peeled himself away from the counter. 'I got your gold outside.'

Starr blinked. 'Gold . . . what do you mean?'

Caleb was walking to the door. The bank manager had no option but to follow. Caleb stumbled slightly as he went to the rear of the wagon, then he recovered and pulled open the tailgate. The bank manager stared incredulously at the stacked gold.

'My God!' He looked beyond the gold bars and saw two little faces peering out at him. 'And you brought back the children also.'

'Hold it! Hold it right there! I got you covered. Step away from the wagon,

Starr. Blood, turn round and keep your hands in sight.'

Slowly Caleb turned. Sheriff LeMoyne was standing in the road, feet astride and a pistol levelled at the men at the back of the wagon.

'Sheriff LeMoyne, put up that gun at once.' To his credit Starr stepped in front of Caleb as he called out to the lawman. 'This man has recovered the stolen gold.'

'Keep away from the suspect, Starr. Blood, toss your gun out into the street.'

'Sheriff! This is nonsense. Mr Blood had brought me back my gold. He has also rescued the two missing children.'

'I'll shoot if I have to. Whatever cock-and-bull story he's cooked up it's a lie. I know these Bloods. The whole family are scum. So stand back and let me handle this.'

'Caleb!'

Crystal was running down the street from the direction of the Horn of Plenty.

'Stand back, ma'am!' the sheriff yelled. 'This is an armed stand-off. I'll shoot if I have to.'

But Crystal was not to be stopped. She ran past the lawman and flung her arms around Caleb.

'Oh, Caleb . . . Caleb . . . ' She was weeping and stroking his face at the same time.

'Auntie Crystal! Auntie!'

'Oh Caleb, it's Gale and little Caleb.'

Crystal was trying to hold on to Caleb and reach into the wagon towards the children.

'You are the best of men, Caleb Blood. I love you.' She sobbed. 'I love you all.'

18

Caleb Blood was swimming up from the deep and dark waters of the vortex. As he neared the surface a brilliant white light appeared above him. He stared in wonderment at the fiery object suspended over the water. It was in the shape of a cross but a cross of such burnished brightness it hurt his eyes to look at it. A figure bent from the cross towards him and held out a hand. Just as he was about to take hold of the hand the vision faded.

'Caleb, wake up.'

He surfaced and saw someone bent over him shaking him gently.

'Crystal.'

'It's about time. You've been asleep twelve hours. I was getting worried. Are you all right?'

He gazed up at her and then past her, not recognizing the room. 'Where am I?'

'We're in the Pirouette Hotel.' She suddenly smiled. 'You got the best room in the hotel.'

He was frowning trying to gather his thoughts, wondering what the dream was about with the glowing cross and the hand reaching out.

'You're a hero, Caleb, and rich to boot. When the bank was robbed and the posse returned empty-handed Starr offered a reward of five thousand dollars for the return of the gold. Then you turn up with it and he has to pay you the reward.'

He eased himself up in the bed, trying to clear his head.

'I been asleep twelve hours, did you say?'

'You fell down in the street. Starr had men carry you in here. At first we thought you were wounded but couldn't find any holes in you.'

He was silent, thinking he had been asleep all that time and the black dream had not disturbed him. No burning church, no screaming, no hurting.

'The children, they all right?'

A shadow crossed her face. 'The poor mites, seems I was right. When the shooting started they hid in the wagon. It was only when the bandits got back to their hideout that they were discovered. It must have been terrifying.' She was silent a moment. 'Then I had to tell them their mammy was gone. It like to broke my heart to see their little faces. I'd rather jump in a frozen lake than have to do that again. But they're staying at the hotel and with everything being new and different it maybe distracts them a little.

'I brought you a bottle, Caleb.' She indicated the bedside table. 'Thought maybe you might like a drink when you woke.'

For a long time he stared at the bourbon nestling only a few feet from him. A faint tremor went through him. It was Crystal's turn to be silent now, watching him.

'I'm hungry, where are my clothes?' he asked.

'I reckon Len Jackson oughta go in Musgrave and find out where that son of a bitch is,' James Vance opined. 'I don't think either Hardy or myself should show our faces in there. Someone might just remember us from when we stayed there last.'

Jackson, tall and lean, smiled. 'Reckon I can ride in, have myself a fling with the fillies and then drift back out again.'

The four outlaws were camped a few miles from the town, debating their next moves. They had trailed the wagon this far and were puzzled as to why the man who had hijacked their gold would go back to the very place from where it had been stolen.

'That Blood is a clever bastard. I reckon that sonabitch is gonna hide that gold till the heat dies down, then light out with it and no one the wiser,' Hardy put in. 'We steal the gold and he gets to keep it. Damnit, I want that sonabitch in my sights. You shoulda let me kill him that night.'

'For Gawd's sake, Hardy, you say

that one more time an' you and I will be slapping leather,' Vance snapped. 'You're like an old woman with your nagging.'

Hardy stared hard at his partner. 'You wanna match irons with me just say the word and you can have your chance.'

'Aw hell,' Broody, the dark-bearded bandit intervened. 'Can you two save your fighting till we get our hands on that gold. Then if'n you kill each other that'll leave more gold for Jackson an' me.'

By the time Jackson got into Musgrave it was dusk. He could find no one at the livery so he left his horse in the corral at the rear of the stables and walked down to the nearest saloon.

With a whiskey in his hand he mingled with the men drinking and gambling. In short time he was in a poker game. The stakes were fairly small and being a careful man he played cautiously.

'Heard you had a little excitement around here a few days back,' he ventured after a few hands.

'Excitement!' A bald man in a suit exclaimed. 'I should say so. Had enough excitement to see this town into the next century.'

'Yeah, heard tell a bunch of fellas robbed the bank. Did they get away with much?'

'Gold bullion it was. Goddamn bank won't disclose how much but they were able to offer a five-thousand-dollar reward.'

Jackson whistled. 'Five thousand! That'd set up a fella for life. Might have a crack at finding that gold myself.'

There were chuckles all round the table.

'We can tell you where it's at, stranger, if you wanna have a go at getting your hands on it.'

'Oh, yeah! How's that?'

'Shall we tell him, boys?'

His fellow gamblers were grinning as they relished the stranger's confusion. The man in the suit leaned confidentially towards Jackson.

'That there gold is back in the bank'

The card-players howled gleefully at the astonished look on Jackson's face.

'You're joshing me.'

'No siree, young Caleb Blood, he went out and recovered that there gold and brought it right back here to Percy Starr, the bank manager. Near got himself arrested, too. Sheriff LeMoyne from Newtown was here looking into the robbery, though the only thing he was looking into was a whiskey jar. Starr had a helluva job persuading LeMoyne not to arrest Blood. LeMoyne reckoned Caleb was in on the bank robbery. Seems there's some history between them. Reckons Blood's a bad 'un'.

Jackson spent the night in the arms of a willing female, then trailed back to camp late next morning to relate the bad news to his companions.

★　★　★

Caleb climbed down from the wagon and went to the entrance of the burial parlour. The undertaker was waiting for Caleb and shook hands with him.

'I've done what you instructed, Mr Blood. Mrs Blood is embalmed and the coffin is ready to be loaded.'

A small crowd had gathered when they saw the wagon draw up at the undertakers. Caleb stood on the board-walk and watched the men carry the coffin out and load it into the wagon. The two children sat solemnly on the front seat. They had said their farewells to Crystal when they left the hotel. There had been tears and hugs from Crystal for Caleb and the children.

'And don't worry about the funeral service. Mr Tomb, my colleague in Newtown, will take care of everything for you.' The undertaker shook Caleb's hand once more. 'Goodbye, Mr Blood. It is a sorrowful duty you now embark upon but one that is bound up with our Christian duty. It is a credit to you that you wish to unite your brother and his wife in death. I'm sure they are united already in the bosom of the Lord. May God go with you.'

19

'I guess we might as well go out to the ranch. Would you like that?'

Gale and little Caleb stared solemnly back at him. They still treated him with guarded reserve. Not having any experience of children he was unaware his fierce, unkempt appearance was intimidating to the youngsters. Added to this they were still traumatized by the death of their mother and their abduction by the gang of bank robbers. He did his best to get along with them and though they clung to him it was because he was all they had.

It had been his intention to leave the children at the hotel while he interred their mother in the town cemetery. But when he proposed this they had become distressed. With careful questioning he realized they were fearful they would lose him as they had lost their parents. Apart from Crystal, whom they had left behind in Musgrave, he was the only person linked to their father and mother. In the end he had taken them with him.

The Newtown undertaker performed the funeral with solemnity and respect. Caleb had stood by the grave of his brother and, not for the first time, wondered how it was that Charlie was dead while he, Caleb, still lived.

'It ain't fair, Charlie. You did something with your life. You had a family to live for. I would willingly swap places with you if that were possible. But I promise I'll do my best to look after your kids for you.'

As he whispered these words he was suddenly hit by the extent of his responsibilities. What did he know about children? All he had ever known was war and killing.

He had ridden out from Musgrave after the bank robbers purely with the intention of rescuing his niece and nephew. Then he had encountered the man he held responsible for the terrible crimes committed in Perryville. When he reached for his Colt hidden in the saddlebags it was not to kill but to hold the outlaws at bay. Once the gun was in his hand something in him had changed.

Images of the women and children burned alive in the church; Marty, lying dead in the street and Elvira shot in her bed rose in his mind. And suddenly the Colt became an instrument of retribution. He regretted those actions but that was all in the past and there would be no need for any more killing.

'OK, then I'll go and hitch up the wagon.'

'Can we come with you?'

They had come back to the hotel after the funeral. Caleb figured he would go out to the ranch just to look the place over and then, if the children were agreeable, they would start back in the morning for Musgrave.

'Come on then.' Caleb was pleased the children seemed less wary of him.

'We'll hitch up Caesar. I'm sure he'll be glad to see his old home again.'

He had no sooner stepped out from the hotel than he stopped. Three cowboys were standing by the doorway. Caleb recognized them immediately: Mathew Hecht and his henchmen were blocking the boardwalk.

'Well, well, look what we got here. Caleb Blood suddenly pops up like a goddamn bad smell. I run you outta town once, Blood. Why'd you come back?'

'Go back in the hotel and wait for me,' Caleb ordered the children. A small hand was slipped into his. He looked down. Gale was holding tight to him, her little body was trembling. 'It's all right, Gale. Just go back inside.'

'I don't want those bad men to hurt you.'

There was a snort of laughter from Hecht. 'Ain't that a touching sight. Cowardly Caleb Blood hiding behind his brother Charlie's brats.'

'I don't want no trouble, Hecht. I

just came back to bury Elvira and Charlie. I'll be gone by tomorrow.'

Hecht was shaking his head. 'No, you won't be gone tomorrow. You are going now, pronto, today.'

The confrontation was attracting a small crowd.

Caleb gently released his hand from Gale. 'Please, Gale, go inside the hotel.'

Slowly she backed away but stopped in the doorway of the hotel. He glanced around for his nephew and blinked in surprise. Little Caleb was standing in front of the Box MH foreman, his tiny fists clenched.

'You leave my Uncle Caleb alone,' his little voice piped out.

Caleb moved up to his nephew and bent over him to pull the child to safety. As he placed his hands on his nephew Hecht roughly slapped the boy out of the way and punched Caleb.

Caleb staggered sideways into the hitching rail in front of the hotel. Completely off balance he crashed helplessly into the rail, breaking the structure as he crashed through and pitched on to the road. As he hit the dirt he heard Gale screaming.

Caleb rolled to his knees and shook his head to clear it. The screaming of his niece was loud and piercing. For a moment he had the illusion he was kneeling in front of a burning church, powerless to help the screaming children inside.

Hecht jumped off the boardwalk, landed beside Caleb and booted him viciously. Caleb grunted as the pain jolted through his body. Gale was still screaming and mingled with it was the sobs of little Caleb.

Caleb was lying in the road amongst the pieces of broken rail: stout wooden poles nailed together to form a tethering place for horses. He could hear the children screaming. The boot hit him again. This time he was ready.

Caleb grabbed the boot and twisted savagely. Hecht yelled and fell heavily. Caleb saw Hecht's buddies jumping from the boardwalk to join in the fight.

As he came to his feet he scooped up a length of broken rail. In one fluid movement he smashed the rail across the face of the nearest man. The gunman went back, arms flailing.

His companion, seeing his buddy go down, made a grab for his six-gun. Caleb swiped hard with the rail and the blow broke the man's arm. He fell back cursing, his gun tumbling into the dirt.

In the meantime Hecht was recovering and coming to his feet. Caleb swung his improvised club hard and fast at the foreman. Hecht threw up hands to ward off the blow and the rail smashed into his elbow. Hecht yelled, as the joint was shattered. He clawed for his weapon with his good hand.

Caleb was too fast. He swung the rail and broke the other wrist, and again a gun dropped to the dirt. Hecht was backing away, a frightened look on his face, but Caleb was not finished yet. He went after the injured man, raining blows mercilessly on the unfortunate Box MH foreman.

Suddenly a shot rang out and something burned along Caleb's ribs. Forgetting his battered victim for the time being Caleb dropped to the roadway as if the bullet had seriously injured him. Intentionally he landed close to Hecht's fallen Colt. With one swift movement he grabbed up the weapon. Hecht's gunman was standing by the boardwalk, lining up his weapon for another shot at Caleb. Caleb's Colt was coming up fast. He triggered off a shot.

The gunman staggered back, a surprised look on his face. He put his hand to his chest and looked down at the blood pumping through his fingers. The wounded man was still holding his gun. Caleb waited, Hecht's gun in his hand ready. The gunman tried to bring up his weapon. Caleb shot him again and this time the man went over backwards, crashing to the boardwalk. His legs kicked for a moment, then he was still.

Caleb remembered Hecht and swivelled

on his heel to cover the Box MH man. As he moved another shot rang out. Caleb felt a savage blow on his shoulder that spun him around again. As he dropped to the dirt he glimpsed a figure beyond Hecht with a smoking pistol. He fired instinctively.

The man jerked and stepped back, trying to bring his gun to bear on Caleb. Caleb did not hesitate. He fired again and a red mushroom of blood suddenly appeared in the man's throat. His mouth worked feverishly for seconds, blood erupting from his lips, then he collapsed into the roadway. Caleb slowly stood up, scanning the street, alert for more gunmen. He heard someone yelling.

'It's Sheriff LeMoyne! Someone's shot Sheriff LeMoyne!'

20

Caleb ignored the shouting and walked slowly in the direction of the fallen lawman. He was not too concerned about shooting a man who was trying to kill him, whether he was a lawman or anyone else. He could feel the shoulder hurting now and blood pumping from the wound.

Hecht was standing helplessly by the sheriff's body, staring down at the dead man. He sensed the movement near him and turned. His face, already pale from his injuries, went a shade whiter when he saw who was advancing towards him.

Caleb reached the foreman. He was still carrying Hecht's gun which had helped him survive the two attempts on his life. When he got to Hecht he slowly brought the weapon up and placed it against the man's temple. Hecht folded at the knees and kneeled in front of Caleb.

'Please, please don't kill me. I'm sorry. We didn't mean any harm. It was just a bit of funning.'

Caleb kept the gun against the terrified man's head. Hecht closed his eyes, sweat pouring down his face. Caleb noticed a fat man with a badge cautiously coming up towards them. He kept a wary eye on the newcomer as he spoke to the man kneeling before him.

'Elvira told me things that suggest to me that you were involved in my brother's murder.'

'Oh God, please!' Hecht was bent over, not able to look at Caleb. 'It's not true. It was Hawkins and Jacobs. I tried to stop them.'

Caleb blinked and looked up at the fat man. The lawman said nothing, waiting, staring at the cringing Hecht.

'Hawkins and Jacobs?' Caleb said. 'Those two apes back there?'

'That's them. I swear I tried to stop them. They were wild on drink. There was nothing I could do.'

Blood was pouring down Caleb's arm but he ignored it. He looked up at the fat lawman waiting.

'Deputy Hardin,' the man introduced himself. 'I heard what he said. You want me to arrest them?'

Caleb closed his eyes, briefly feeling dizzy, then opened them again.

'I don't care one way or the other. It won't bring Charlie back. You do what you think.' He turned his attention back to the kneeling man. 'That's the second time you ordered me out of town, Hecht, and it's the last. Whether the deputy arrests you or not for the murder of my brother makes no difference. Now I'm telling you, get out of Newtown. Get out of the territory. When next I meet you, I'll shoot you on sight.'

Deputy Hardin stepped back and watched as Hecht clambered to his feet and shuffled off down the street. The lawman made no move to stop him. He had his thumbs tucked in his belt. His head turned and he spat a gob of tobacco juice that landed between the sprawled legs of the dead sheriff.

'LeMoyne! He shot me.' Caleb indicated the blood dripping from his arm and making tiny blobs in the dust of the road. 'It was self-defence.'

The crowd of onlookers was growing. Deputy Hardin turned to them.

'Some of you fellas take the sheriff down to the morgue.' He waved a hand towards the front of the hotel where the other body lay. 'You shoot him too?'

' 'Fraid so.'

'I need more volunteers to carry that other body as well.'

Men were coming forward.

'I'll need you to come down the jail and make a statement.'

Caleb watched the citizens of Newtown carting away the dead. 'Are you arresting me?'

The deputy shrugged. 'I watched it all. LeMoyne was acting strange, keeping an eye on the hotel, so I kept an eye on him. I sorta got the feeling he was waiting for the fight to happen. He didn't intervene till he saw you were getting the better of Hecht and his pals.'

Caleb stared back at the deputy, thinking about what he said and what was left unsaid.

'I got two small children need tending.'

'You do that. Come down see me when you're ready.' The deputy spat again. 'That means there's a vacancy for the job of sheriff. Don't suppose you'd put yourself forward?'

Caleb looked up in surprise. The fat cheeks of the deputy creased in a smile.

'I just heard Hecht more or less confess to the murder of Charlie Blood. I reckon everybody knew who killed Charlie, including Sheriff LeMoyne, but he was too far up Mitchell Houseman's ass to want to do anything about it. You're obviously handy with a gun. You could maybe clear up a few more mysterious killings around here.'

'Can I go see to my kids?'

'You need that wound seeing to. Where are you staying? I'll send the sawbones to you.'

Caleb flicked his head back towards the hotel. Before he could say anything he saw two small figures running towards him. Little arms wrapped themselves around his waist. He looked down at the tearful faces.

'Uncle Caleb, you're hurt.'

'It's OK, Gale. It's only a scratch.'

'I guess you must be Caleb Blood?'

Caleb looked up when he heard the deputy's query. 'I guess,' he said warily.

'You're the fella as recovered the stolen gold back in Musgrave. I heard all about that, Mr Blood. I sure admire what you did.' The deputy spat on the road where the body of his boss had lain. 'This fool sheriff reckoned you stole the gold and then brought it back to claim the reward.' He chuckled. 'Heard he wanted to arrest you.'

Caleb smiled grimly. 'I knew nothing about it. That musta been after I passed out.'

Hardin roared with laughter. He turned, the sound of his mirth fading as he walked back towards the jailhouse. The children were holding on to Caleb and it was with difficulty he managed to turn around and head towards the hotel.

'Let's get inside, kids.'

There was no sign of the dead gunman, who had obviously been hauled away by Hardin's volunteers. Of the third man there was no sign either. Only the wrecked hitching rail gave indication of the violence that had just occurred. With his niece and nephew clinging to him Caleb climbed wearily up the hotel steps.

'I guess we'll havta postpone our trip to the ranch till another day.'

They were in the lobby. The manager, a small balding man with large mutton-chop whiskers watched timidly as the bloodied man and his children entered.

'Deputy Hardin is sending the doc over to patch up my wound,' Caleb told him. 'Send him up to my room when he arrives.'

'Sure thing, Mr Blood.' The manager was staring with horror at the blood dripping on the lobby floor.

'Sorry about the mess. I'll pay for any extra clean-up.'

At this point the manager disappeared from view, flopping down behind the desk in a crumpled heap, the sight of blood on his lobby floor too much for him. Caleb peered behind the desk.

'I guess the doc can tend to you at the same time,' he said to the unconscious man. 'Though I'd recommend smelling-salts myself.'

'Is he dead, Uncle Caleb?'

His nephew was staring up at him, his face pale.

'Hey, that was some fight you put up out there,' he said remembering the little fellow squaring up to Hecht. 'If it weren't for you, them fellas mighta got the better of me.'

Little Caleb's face stared earnestly up

at his uncle. 'But he knocked me down.' As he said this he let go Caleb's hand and rubbed the side of his head where Hecht had hit him.

'Yeah, that was a good trick on your part. It gave me a chance to break up that hitching rail and use it as a weapon. If you hadn't distracted him all three woulda jumped me and I wouldn't have stood a chance.'

Little Caleb's face brightened as he thought this over.

'Yeah, I reckon.'

'Uncle Caleb, are you gonna die?' It was Gale who captured her uncle's attention now.

'Naw, this is just a little hole in my shoulder. It'll heal up quick.'

The truth was more painful as he felt the burning in his shoulder where the bullet had hit.

'I don't want you to die. Mummy and Daddy died. If you die there'll be no one to take care of us no more, excepting Miss Crystal.'

Caleb looked down at the two

worried little faces staring up at him.

'You like Miss Crystal, then?'

'She's a fine lady. Are you going to marry her?'

Her uncle was saved from answering with the arrival of the doctor.

21

'You stupid piece of goddamn horse manure!' Mitchell Houseman, owner of the Box MH, raged at his foreman. 'The three of you along with Sheriff LeMoyne couldn't handle one goddamn whiskey soak?'

Hecht squirmed under the lash of his boss's tongue, the arm with his ruined elbow in a sling and bandages on his other arm. His face was drawn and pale and he was obviously in much pain from his injuries.

'Hell, boss, he took us by surprise. He was lying in wait for us. He shot Hawkins, then made us take off our guns and laid into us with a pickaxe handle. Mighta beat us to death too, only Sheriff LeMoyne arrived and tried to arrest him. Blood just shot him down without warning. While he was shooting it out with LeMoyne we made our escape.'

'What a mess! What a goddamn fine mess this is!' Houseman stood looking with contempt at the injured man. 'You ain't much use to me now with two busted wings. Get the hell outta my sight.'

The disgraced foreman stumbled from the room, glad to escape from his boss's anger. In his haste he blundered into Houseman's wife as she was about to enter the room.

'Hecht,' she exclaimed. 'What on earth . . . ?'

The disgraced foreman did not answer, intent only on escaping from the enraged Houseman.

'Most extraordinary.'

Mrs Houseman pushed inside the room that Hecht had just vacated so hastily. Her husband was in the act of lighting a large cigar.

'What on earth's going on, Mitchell? I've almost been knocked over by Mathew Hecht. He looked most upset. What did you say to him?'

'Huh, that feeble excuse for a man! I

sent him into town to help Sheriff LeMoyne send that Blood fellow packing. Now he comes back here with his tail between his legs and LeMoyne shot to boot.'

Alice Houseman's face set into a tight frown. 'You mean Caleb Blood has returned to Newtown?'

Her husband eyed her through clouds of cigar smoke. 'I hadn't told you before as I thought Hecht would deal with him and chase him back to whatever hole he crawled outta.'

Now in her middle years, Alice Houseman was still a handsome woman with a fine figure and a face unlined by age, but now that face took on a hard and calculating look as she thought over this piece of news regarding Caleb Blood.

'You know Laura's due back any day now with her fiancé?'

'You don't have to tell me. That was one reason I set Hecht on to Blood. It all backfired and Blood got the jump on him and killed LeMoyne into the bargain. Until I get a new sheriff in place it seems Blood is free to wander at will around Newtown.'

'He killed LeMoyne! Dear God, what's the world coming to? But surely Deputy Hardin has arrested Blood?'

'That fat swill-belly! I might as well have a pork hog for law officer as that big-bellied loon. LeMoyne hated having to work with that lard-assed knuckle-head. But we couldn't get rid of him, as he is cousin to the governor.'

'I must say I always thought Hardin was an odious character, what with chewing that disgusting tobacco and spitting. And he had no respect for his betters, either.'

'Well, we're stuck with him for the time being.' Mitchell began to pace up and down. 'The thing is we gotta find out what Blood's intending to do. The reason he came back was to bury Elvira Blood, or so we're led to believe. With luck he might just move on now he's done that.'

'What about the Blood ranch? I

thought you were trying to get your hands on that?'

'I have my lawyer Cassidy on it at the moment. He thinks we can buy up the bank notes and take over the place. But it all takes time. Until the will is read and the estate settled we're just marking time. But don't worry, my dear. Caleb Blood is a waster and a whiskey-hound. If the ranch is legally Caleb's he'll want to sell up, take the money and run. If the worst comes to the worst I'll have Cassidy make him an offer for the ranch. Then he'll be out of our hair.'

'Mitchell, I don't want him about when Laura arrives back home. I don't want that to start all over again. It took a lot of doing to separate them before. What if she's still harbouring feelings for Blood?'

'Alice, that was years ago. Laura was just an impressionable young girl. She's been back East and had an education. There's no way she'll want to rekindle any kind of relationship with that bum.

Hell, word is he's living with a whore back in Musgrave. If Laura even remembers Blood we'll soon put her right about what kind of miscreant he's turned out to be. In the meantime, just to be on the safe side, I'll set the wheels in motion to have him arrested for killing a lawman.'

Alice Houseman's eyes narrowed and her face was set in a hard mask as she glared at her husband. 'Mitchell Houseman, you make sure you do what is necessary to keep that piece of dirt away from my daughter. She deserves better. Now she has found a good man we have to make sure we keep her secure. The Bloods are low-down trash. I'd rather see my daughter dead and buried than mixed up with that Caleb Blood.' Her voice was dripping with venom as she spoke. 'You bear that in mind, Mitchell Houseman. I don't care what it takes or how many people you have to bribe or how many guns you have to hire, just you make sure Caleb Blood and

Laura Houseman never meet up again.'

'Don't worry, my dear. Our daughter is as precious to me as she is to you. I have no intention of allowing old flames to be rekindled. One way or the other I will rid us of Caleb Blood.'

★ ★ ★

The outlaws rode into Newtown just before the sun went down. They stabled their horses at the livery and drifted down to the Globe saloon to wet their whistles and get a sense of what was happening in the town. The main object of their enquiries was the man who had hijacked the gold from the bank robbery and murdered their comrades.

The men split up to circulate amongst the drinkers and find out what they could about their target. It was not long before they had the information they required. Caleb Blood was the main subject of almost every conversation. In a very short time the four outlaws gathered together in order to compare notes.

'That son of a bitch is here all right. The whole town is talking about him. The goddamn son of a bitch only went and killed the sheriff in a shoot-out.'

'Yeah, shot him this afternoon out there in the street.'

Tom Hardy grunted. 'What is it with this guy? He riles me back in Musgrave an' I beat the sawdust outta him. He just lies there taking it. Then I was about to put a few holes in his hide and let some of the whiskey leak out, only that saloon owner stopped me. I went easy on him cos Vance tells me.

'Next thing he's trailed Harwinton to the hideout — shoots the living daylights outta our boys and takes our gold. Now he's come here and shoots a sheriff. According to everyone he walked away from that shooting scot free.' He shook his head in disgust.

'He seems to have the luck of the devil all right,' James Vance put forward. 'The only way we're gonna get the better of that rattlesnake is to lie in wait for him some night an' bushwhack him. We need to find out what he's done with the reward money he got from the bank. I want something back for all the trouble we went to robbing that bank. I suggest we hang around town and watch that sonabitch. Once we know his habits we'll grab him, make him tell us where the money is and then kill him.'

'I reckon,' agreed Hardy. 'But let's not wait too long. I can't wait for the pleasure of beating the hell outta him afore we kill him.'

22

The coach bumped and swayed along the uneven highway, shaking the passengers and kicking up a light dust that powdered everything on the outside and to a lesser extent inside as well. Kurt Wyman smiled across at the young woman sitting opposite. Laura Houseman and he were travelling together but Wyman had insisted they sit opposite each other.

'So as I can look at you as we travel to your home. That way I shall be reminded what a lucky fellow I am to be in love with the most beautiful girl ever to come out of the West.'

His forthright compliments had the ability to make her blush no matter how many times she heard them. During the journey, each time she caught his eye he smiled faintly reminding her of his professed adoration. Sitting beside Kurt

Wyman was his constant companion, Duane Harper.

There were three other passengers in the coach besides Laura and her two male companions, a drummer who dozed throughout most of the journey, clutching his case of samples and muttering under his breath when the coach hit a particularly deep pothole and jolted him awake. A plump woman and a young girl who was obviously her daughter made up the last two passengers.

Laura was excited and happy and also a little apprehensive now that she was at last going home. Not only was she going home but also she was bringing back the man she was to marry.

Just eighteen years old, Laura Houseman gave off a glow of health and vitality. She had reddish-gold hair and a tawny colouring that reminded one of a golden eagle. Like the eagle she was bright, alert and gifted with the ability to soar far above the world of ordinary mortals. At least that was the impression she conveyed, and men either stood in awe of her or fell madly in love.

The man she was to marry was much older than Laura. Fast approaching his late thirties Kurt Wyman had a frank, open face with wide-spaced eyes that sometimes appeared blue and sometimes grey and on occasion dark and brooding. He was dressed in a suit, for Wyman was a businessman with interests in railroad developments.

If anything could be said to spoil Laura's enjoyment travelling in the company of Kurt Wyman it was the man who accompanied them and who in fact was never far away from the engaged couple.

Duane Harper had the ability to make Laura feel uneasy every time he looked at her. It was nothing Harper ever said or did, for he very seldom addressed himself to her; it was the aura of sinister menace the man gave off.

Harper had dark, bottomless eyes set in a lean face with regular features. He would have been considered handsome but for the perpetual menacing scowl that marred his countenance.

Duane Harper was bodyguard to Kurt Wyman. A gunman of extraordinary skill, he was an invaluable asset to a ruthless businessman who had made many enemies on his way to the top of his profession. As a railroad baron Kurt Wyman had of necessity ridden roughshod over many a farmer and rancher who stood in his way.

When land rights were required for expansion it was Wyman who managed to persuade reluctant landowners to sell at a knockdown price to the railroad. Shareholders did not enquire too closely into Wyman's business methods. They were only too keen to take advantage of the amazing deals he seemed able to wring out of even the most reluctant tenants who stood in the way of progress.

Without the presence of the gunman

Laura Houseman's trip home with her fiancé would have been more comfortable. But she was young and in love and so she glossed over the many little flaws in the man she was to marry. Had she been older and wiser maybe some of the things she observed might just have given her pause for thought.

The coach trip was the last leg of the journey from Boston, where Laura had spent the last couple of years. The rail link had not been built as far as Newtown, which necessitated travelling the final part by coach.

Laura had been living with relatives in Boston while she attended college. She was slightly apprehensive of introducing Kurt to her folk, wondering whether he would find them too unsophisticated for his Eastern manners. And so she spent the few hours of the coach trip rehearsing her meeting with her parents and the task of presenting her fiancé to them.

The coach was labouring up a steep gradient. Laura could hear the driver swearing at the horses and the crack of the whip as he urged his team to greater efforts.

'Come on you goddamn fleabags! I pull my pecker harder than you goddamn mules are pulling.' The swearing was punctuated by the crack of the whip as it whistled out over the backs of the sweating, labouring horses. 'I reckon you lot are fit only for the slaughterhouse, you goddamn lazy crook-backed bags of bones.'

The other female passenger looked disconcerted and glanced distractedly at her daughter as the swearing penetrated to the interior of the coach. Laura smiled in sympathy at the young mother. Having been brought up on her father's ranch, listening to the ranch hands' irreverent swearing from an early age, she was used to the rough ways of horsemen and the coarse manner with which they encouraged their animals to greater efforts.

The gunshots when they suddenly blasted out shocked everyone inside the coach into wakeful apprehension. The cussing from outside the coach increased. A voice was heard shouting instructions to the driver. The coach had slowed considerably.

'What the hell, we ain't got nothing you fellas'll be needing!' the driver yelled.

'Shut up and stop those goddamn hosses! Guard, if you don't shuck that shotgun you'll be pushing up daisies in boot hill.'

Laura was arching her head around to peer out of the window. She could see a man on the side of the trail, his face hidden behind a bandanna. He was threatening the men atop the coach with a six-gun. Her eyes widened in alarm.

'It's a hold-up,' she exclaimed. 'There's a masked man on the trail ahead.'

'Throw down the strongbox.'

'Hell, there ain't nothing in there, only mail.'

'Just do as you're told! You rile me any I'll put a bullet in that ornery hide of yours.'

'Hell, I ain't figgering on being shot on this job. The bosses don't pay enough for me to risk my life for the sake of a few dollars as might be in that there box.'

The coach rocked as the guard moved atop the roof to get at the strongbox. Inside, the passengers listened to the noises as the box was dragged to the side and heaved over. A face suddenly appeared alongside the coach and the door was wrenched open.

'Everybody out!'

Nobody moved. A shot suddenly blasted out. making Laura jump. The bullet went somewhere into the roof of the coach.

'You people deaf? I said out!'

The little girl began to cry. Her terrified mother put an arm around her. Laura left her seat and moved to the door. The outlaw had pulled the steps into position and was a few strides away at the side of the track with his pistol pointed into the doorway.

'Stop shooting, we got women and children in here,' she called out.

'Shut up, miss, and just get on down here.'

Laura complied and dropped to the dust on the trail. The rest of the passengers followed her. The driver and guard climbed down off coach to join them on the road. Two more bandits appeared, mounted on horses. One was trailing another mount, which must have belonged to the one now standing by the coach and threatening the passengers with his pistol.

'OK folk, listen carefully.' A gunnysack was produced and waved in the air. 'You gonna empty your pockets and put any valuables into this here gunnysack.'

As the outlaw gave his instructions Duane Harper was moving sideways, away from the group of passengers lining up by the side of the coach.

'Mister, where the hell you think you're going?'

Harper looked at the outlaw without answering, but stopped where he was.

'Harper,' Kurt Wyman yelled excitedly, 'do as the man says!'

As he shouted out Wyman was also moving but in the opposite direction. It was inevitable that all eyes switched towards the railroad boss. There was a flicker of movement from Harper. No one saw the gun appear by some sleight of hand. He did not seem to aim but bullets spewed out in a deadly stream.

His target was the gunman standing before the passengers with the gunnysack. Bullets stitched holes in his chest and he was punched backwards, his legs giving way as he fell to the roadway.

At the same time Kurt Wyman had pulled a weapon and coolly began firing at the horsemen. The outlaws stood no chance. Before they could react they were in a crossfire and mown down as Wyman and Harper performed a well-rehearsed routine taking the bandits off guard. The two mounted outlaws were caught in a hail of lead and died without loosing off a round.

A stunned silence followed the loud

explosions of the handguns. The young woman screamed.

'Oh my God!' the drummer said and slid down the side of the coach to sit in the dirt.

Laura stared with wide-eyed disbelief at the outlaws grotesquely sprawled in death in the dirt. She turned to look at her fiancé. Kurt Wyman was calmly ejecting spent shells from his pistol. He caught her look and smiled grimly.

'It's all right, Laura. You're safe now.'

23

When the stagecoach pulled into Newtown an hour late there were three ponies tied at the rear with the dead bandits lashed atop each beast. As word spread about the hold-up a crowd gathered by the hotel, eager to learn what had happened to the coach. It was the drummer who was the centre of attention, for he was the one willing to talk about the incident.

A Box MH carriage was waiting for the arrival of the stagecoach. Without wasting any time Kurt Wyman had their luggage loaded and, ignoring all questions from the citizens of Newtown, instructed the cowboy in the driving seat to take them immediately to the ranch, leaving the drummer to regale the crowd with the gory details of the foiled hold-up.

'Greased lightning, those two fellas,'

he claimed. 'Them bandits had their irons in their hands holding us there while they were robbing us. Not only did they want the strongbox but also they wanted all our personal possessions. That Wyman fella weren't having none of his stuff stolen.'

'Wyman, is that the fella in the suit?' someone in the crowd enquired.

'That's him, the tall good-looking one with the straw-coloured hair. His partner is Duane Harper, the gunfighter. Well, Harper might be fast but that Wyman weren't a cat's whisker behind him.'

'Duane Harper, I heard of him. He's from Texas, ain't he?'

'That's right, he was a Texas Ranger for a time but they reckoned he was killing too many innocent people so he was drummed outta the force.'

'Whoopee!' a young cowboy yelled. 'No wonder them hold-up men didn't stand a chance. Wish I'da been there to see that.'

'I tell you, man, I was so piss-scared I

like to have fainted,' the drummer admitted.

By this time the dead bandits had been carted down to the mortuary. Many were the invites for the drummer to join some of the crowd down the Silver Sphere saloon. It took little persuasion for him to agree. Now that the main protagonists had been spirited away to the Box MH the drummer was the only source of first-hand information. Indeed the man was wallowing in the reflected glory of the men who had foiled a hold-up and wiped out the bandit gang in the process.

Laura Houseman was in a state of shock. The bewildering efficiency with which her fiancé and his bodyguard had exterminated the gang distressed her. It had all been done with the minimum of effort and lack of emotion on the part of the two men.

After the killing Wyman had taken control of the situation, advising the driver and the shotgun guard to load the bodies of the outlaws on to their horses in order to transport them the last few miles into town.

'Laura,' her father greeted her as she was helped from the carriage. 'We were getting worried. What kept you?'

'Oh Pa, the stagecoach was held up by bandits,' Laura blurted. 'It was horrible.'

By this time the numbness was wearing off and she felt near to tears, but somehow held back now that she had the task of introducing her male companions.

'Pa, this is Kurt Wyman and his . . . ' Laura hesitated, unsure how to introduce a man who was obviously a professional hired gun, 'his associate, Mr Duane Harper.'

The handshakes were brisk and hard as the men weighed each other up. Mitchell Houseman, a shrewd judge of men, quickly assessed Wyman as a tough and sharp operator. Harper he shelved in his mind as a hired gun and dangerous. They entered the house where Alice Houseman was waiting with refreshments for the new arrivals. Small talk was dominated by the news of the attempted stick-up and the fatal consequences for the robbers.

'Hell and damnation, I sure woulda liked to have seen that bit of shooting. Three hold-up men and their guns out and you and Mr Harper still got the drop on them. That was some slick operation. Where'd you learn to shoot like that, Mr Wyman?'

'Call me Kurt; I'm not one for formalities. I served in the war as a colonel. I was one of the few officers who led from the front,' Wyman averred, which was a lie for Wyman had spent the war buying shoddily produced weapons and selling them to the Confederate troops, thereby making his first fortune. 'A man learns very quickly how to survive in the crucible of war or he does not live to tell the tale. But don't read too much into your daughter's telling of the tale. It was more good luck on our part and incompetence on the bandits' part that we were successful in thwarting the hold-up.'

'It's a real pleasure to have you here, Kurt. I hope you enjoy your stay. Anything we can do to further your enjoyment while here, just ask. If you ride, there's saddle horses aplenty, or if you prefer a buggy we can supply that as well.'

'That sure is mighty kind of you, Mitchell. I know the main reason for my visit is to meet my future in-laws but there is also an element of business associated with my trip. My company is looking to expand the railroad out in this direction and I've been asked to do a preliminary survey to suss out the most likely route for the line. Perhaps some of your hands can escort me around the country so as I can get a fair idea of the route we'd be most liable to use.'

'No one knows this country better than my pretty young daughter. I'm sure Laura will be only too eager to have the chance to show you the range she grew up on. You'll find here the finest country, the finest people, and the finest cattle. You'll fall in love with this place. As far as this family is concerned this is God's own country and that's a fact!'

'Mitchell, if you and your lovely wife are anything to go by then every boast you just made is entirely justified.'

24

Caleb Blood drove the wagon on a well-remembered trail to his dead brother's ranch. When he got to the broken wire fencing he did not stop. He recalled, from Elvira's version of events on the night of Charlie's death, it was somewhere hereabouts she had found her husband's battered body.

Before setting out there had been an argument between the children as to who would sit next to Uncle Caleb on the driver's seat. Caleb had resolved the dilemma by seating one each side of him. He could feel their warm little bodies nestled close against him. It gave him a tender feeling of responsibility alien to him, for all his life he had done things independently of others, never worrying about the consequences of his actions. It was a weird feeling to think he was responsible for these two little beings.

He did feel tender and protective towards Charlie's children, and in some way it negated the feelings of guilt that had haunted him in recent years, when the black dream of the burning church descended upon him. Since the rescue of Gale and little Caleb from the outlaw camp and his foreswearing of alcohol the nightmares had ceased. There was no way he wanted them to start up again. He shuddered to think what he had become under the whiskey miasma.

The ranch house came into view and he sensed the children grow solemn and quiet as the wagon plodded closer and closer to their old home.

He noticed in the short time the ranch had been empty everything had become neglected and overgrown. Weeds had sprouted up in the garden that had once been Elvira's responsibility.

'Whoa there,' he called unnecessarily, for Caesar, that staid old horse, instinctively pulled up outside his one-time home.

Caleb sat staring at the front of the building, wondering what it must be like for the two children to return to the place where they had grown up with a mother and father to care for them.

'Right, young 'uns, down you get. First thing I'm gonna do is get some coffee going,' he announced.

Not knowing what he was to find at the ranch he had had the foresight to bring along supplies. He gave the children the task of unloading these and carrying them inside the house. Then, while they were occupied, he unhitched the team and watered them. When he brought back the outlaws' horses he had left them in Musgrave with instructions to sell them and give the proceeds to Marty's dependents. He still had the pinto, which he had named Mart in memory of the livery owner, and the faithful Caesar.

In the kitchen he soon had a pot of coffee on the go.

'What the hell do kids drink?' he wondered. 'I suppose milk. Maybe I can round up some of the cows and milk 'em.'

Suddenly Caleb Blood was hit by the enormous responsibility he now had in looking after two young children. It scared him not a little. He poured coffee and carried the mug back into the living room. Gale was busy tidying and dusting while Caleb was trying to put the leg back on a broken chair, without much success.

'I need a nail and a hammer,' he said looking dolefully at his uncle.

'We'll have a look in the tool shed, Caleb. Perhaps we'll find something in there to mend the chair.'

The boy's face immediately brightened. 'We gotta fix things for Ma and Pa coming home.'

Something squeezed Caleb's insides when he heard this. Gale turned and looked first at her brother and then at her uncle. He stared helplessly back at her. Her little face was solemn as she gazed woefully up at him, then she walked over to her brother and put her arms around him. Little Caleb was blinking at his uncle over his sister's shoulder, bewildered by her sudden show of affection.

'Caleb, Ma and Pa ain't coming back,' Gale said. 'They've gone to heaven.'

Suddenly Caleb was pushing his sister away, disentangling himself from her embrace.

'That's a lie.' Big tears were standing in his eyes. 'You can't say things like that. It ain't true. Why are you telling fibs?'

Caleb stood watching, helpless to move or assist his charges, the lump of dread growing in his stomach.

'Don't be sad, Caleb. Ma and Pa are really happy. They want us to look after things and Uncle Caleb will help.' She turned her distraught face towards him. 'Won't you Uncle Caleb? We can stay here and be a family once more.'

Caleb stared back, unable to speak. It

had not been his intention to stay. He had come out to the ranch to gather a few things for the children and then find someone to look after them. He was a drifter without roots. It had always been so.

Gale's pale little face stared earnestly up at him — trusting. He felt powerless to move, to make a comment that would reassure his dead brother's children.

Gale waited patiently, as only very young children can, confident she had her uncle's support — not saying anything.

He heard the horses then. Suddenly he snapped out of his inertia. He picked up the rifle.

'Stay inside,' he ordered and went to the door.

25

There were three riders, two men and a woman. They came in the yard, wary, watchful, suspicious. He waited, rifle barrel sloping down, not threatening. The strangers pulled up and sat for a moment, not knowing what to make of this shabby, hirsute man with the rifle. He could tell they weren't from around here. One of them wore a suit and he reckoned they were visitors to the area, had maybe lost their way and needed directions.

'Howdy, stranger, we were told this place was empty.'

He was not listening; staring at the woman, not believing his eyes. It was her, slightly older but her just the same. No, not just the same, more beautiful than even he remembered.

'People round here don't like squatters,' the voice, becoming harder. 'Best climb aboard that wagon and keep on moving.'

Still no sign from the scarecrow figure on the porch holding the rifle loosely. Hard to tell where he was looking beneath all that hair. But he was looking at Laura Houseman, the shock of seeing her after all this time temporarily paralysing him. Memories were surfacing, painful memories, recollections and feelings he thought were long ago buried.

'Mister, you deaf or just simple?'

A slight signal from Wyman, and Harper began slowly edging his horse away from his boss, spreading out so the hairy man with the rifle would be between them.

An instinct for sensing changes and movements in men when confronted with unfamiliar situations was nagging at Caleb, giving him the impression of menace from the two horsemen.

'I'm talking to you, boy!' yelled Wyman.

The flicker of movement from the

man to the right of the speaker was sensed rather than seen and Caleb flung himself backwards through the doorway. Bullets scattered splinters from the doorframe where he had stood seconds earlier.

Even as he was falling he triggered a shot at the horseman, not sure if he hit or not, but poking the barrel out and sending more shots winging out, his shoulder hurting where he jarred against the floor. He could see them tugging at reins, trying to wheel their mounts away from the house now that their ambush had failed. Laura was calling out and he held his fire, watching from inside as the horsemen fled from the yard, one of them holding himself folded over in the saddle as if he were hurt.

Laura Houseman was trying to calm her mount spooked by the gunshots. 'Don't shoot! For God's sake stop shooting!' she yelled.

The two horsemen had pulled up several hundred yards from the house, and were now conferring.

'I ain't shooting,' Caleb called. 'Tell them friends of yours if they come around here again shooting innocent folk they'll be toted off in a hearse.'

'I'm sorry. I had no idea they were going to start shooting. Are you all right?'

'What do you think?' He wanted to be angry with her, to say something cutting and cruel, but could not bring himself to do so. 'It'll take more than a couple of city dudes to pull a fast one on me, Missus. Tell your husband he'd be safer off behind a desk than sitting atop a horse and shooting at folk.' He could not resist the last taunt, wondering.

'He's not my husband, at least not yet. I'm riding away now and I'll make them go as well. My name is Laura Houseman. What is your name?'

There was no reply. She waited a while longer, glancing over her shoulder at her companions. Kurt Wyman seemed to be using a handkerchief as a bandage on Duane Harper, winding it round his arm. She rode away then.

He watched her go, infinite sadness washing over him, unwelcome memories coming unbidden of a lost time and a lost innocence.

'Laura,' he whispered and stayed crouched inside the doorway watching the three.

Laura had reached the two men and seemed to be having an argument of some sort with them. Suddenly she wheeled her horse and, using her quirt, spurred away on her own. The men stared after her, then cast glances back towards the house, not seeing Caleb hidden inside watching them. There was some sort of discussion, then the horses were urged on following the direction Laura had taken.

He relaxed then, sitting on the floor just inside the doorway, thinking of all that had just happened, feeling his shoulder throbbing. Wondering who the men were and why they had started shooting.

'Squatter,' he muttered.

'Uncle Caleb,' Gale hissed, recalling him back to the house and his responsibilities and Charlie's kids.

For just a brief moment he wished he had a bottle of bourbon to hide himself in. But immediately he dismissed the idea and heaved himself to his feet.

'It's all right now, kids. Those bad men have gone.'

Gale and Caleb were huddled on the floor beneath the table, looking scared, and he remembered Elvira telling about the men coming and shooting at the house at night after Charlie had been murdered.

Was it those same men with Laura who were responsible for frightening women and children? She seemed genuinely upset that the men had started shooting and had ridden away after arguing with them, as if she did not want to be associated with them and their deeds.

'I won't allow anyone to hurt you,' he

assured them, rising to his feet after one last look to make sure the riders had left. 'What about something to eat?' he moved to his coffee mug and tasted it. 'Ugh, cold,' he complained. 'I guess I need a refresher.'

'Let me get it for you, Uncle Caleb.'

Gale reached for the mug and he let her take it from him, glad to see her recovering from the distressing experience of a few moments ago. Her brother was staring at Caleb wide-eyed, and there was something like hero-worship in the little boy's eyes.

'Those bad men won't kill you the way they killed Ma and Pa,' he asserted.

Caleb hunkered down so his eyes were on a level with the boy. Before he could say anything a pair of arms were wrapped around his neck and little Caleb hugged him hard and tight. Nothing like this had ever happened to Caleb before. Hesitatingly he put his arms around the little body, then he pulled him close.

'There ain't nobody gonna hurt me or you or Gale ever.'

He could feel the little heart beating fast as his nephew hugged him as if he would never let go.

26

She was angry, seething with a red-hot anger. She tongue-lashed Wyman and Harper but mostly her anger was directed at the man she was to marry. He had sat his horse patiently, waiting for the storm to lose its fury, his handsome arrogant face impassive, his pale eyes staring at her expressionless. In the midst of her fury she noticed the bloody bandage tied around Harper's arm.

'You're shot,' she exclaimed as she stared at the blood seeping through the covering.

'It's nothing,' Harper answered, but she could see the anger in him also.

He had tried to murder a man and had failed. Now he bled because that man had been faster and put a bullet into the gunman. How humiliating it must be for him.

'Why?' she cried, 'For God's sake, why?'

'He was getting ready to shoot. We had to stop him.'

But she had seen nothing in the squatter man that had posed a threat. He had carried a weapon, that was true, but didn't almost every man out here go armed? There had been no indication he was about to attack them.

'I don't believe you!' she protested. 'I could understand you shooting the stagecoach robbers, but this man was . . . was harmless.'

'You call this harmless!' Harper held out his wounded arm. 'He shot me.'

'He shot you after you tried to shoot him. You tried to murder him, but why!'

Harper had stared back at her, defiant and she knew then there was no defence for what had happened.

'You're just a killer!' she yelled. She wrenched her horse's head around and fled from them.

Out of sight of her companions she had ridden into an arroyo and dismounted, listening. In a while she heard their horses go by. When she was sure they were well away from her hiding-place she ventured out again and turned her horse back towards the ranch where the shooting scrape had taken place. Cautiously she rode into the yard. There was no sign of anyone.

'Hello the house,' she called and sat her horse, waiting.

The unkempt man came out on the porch. His hair grew in long uncombed strands hiding most of his face. Short stubble covered what was visible of his countenance. In spite of his ragged appearance she had the impression this was a young man.

'You alone?' he asked. He was still carrying the rifle.

Something in his voice evoked memories in her as if she knew it from somewhere in the past.

'Yes, I came back to apologize for what happened. It was inexcusable.'

He said nothing, just remained standing there. She could not see his eyes beneath the hair covering his face.

'My name is Laura Houseman. My father is Mitchell Houseman, the owner of the Box MH.'

'Yeah, I know.'

She waited for more, for him to introduce himself, reveal who it was beneath that impenetrable veil of hair; that mask that hid his features from the world. And still she had that nagging feeling that she should know this creature, had met him somewhere before.

'And you are?' she prompted him.

'I think you should go now. Your friends will be worried about you.'

She waited a moment longer. He stood impassive motionless. For all she knew he was not looking at her but staring off into the distance waiting for her to leave, or searching the area wondering where her two companions were hiding.

'Is there anything I can do to make up for . . . for those men's behaviour?'

'You can ride away from here and

never come back, and tell your boyfriend to stay away also.'

The word boyfriend came out with something like a sneer and she coloured up at the implied slur. To her surprise a small boy emerged from the doorway behind the raggedy man and pushed up against him, his little hand seeking reassurance in the grip of the bigger hand of the man.

'Uncle Caleb, who is that lady?'

She stared at the child, then her gaze lifted to the mask of hair. She was bewildered; her heart started fluttering like a small, trapped bird. There was a giddy light-headedness, an unreal sensation. It seemed the ground shifted slightly and the sky tilted. Her throat was suddenly dry. She swallowed.

He remained impassive, like an ancient tree rooted on the porch, as though the hair had grown like vines and covered up the man.

'Caleb . . . '

It was hardly audible. The name tumbled from her lips like a leaf fallen from a tree, drifting in the air.

There was no response from the man. She was not sure how long the silence stretched between them. She was unable to break into the sudden hush that surrounded them. It was as if the world was watching and held its breath while it waited. The little girl stepping into her view broke the spell.

'Caleb,' Laura said again.

'Hello,' the girl piped out. 'I'm Gale; I'm pleased to meet you.'

He moved then, shaking himself out of the trance that had descended upon him since first seeing her.

'Go in the house. Good day, Miss Laura.'

He shooed the children before him, going inside and closing the door. She sat her horse, a statue on the outside, trembling inside. In a daze she flicked her reins, turned her horse's head around, and headed for the gate out from the yard, not looking back. The horse walked without direction from her, instinctively heading for home. But she did not want to go home; did not want anyone to see her just now.

She urged the horse to a trot and then to a canter. Suddenly she dug in her heels and the horse took off, glad to run. She could feel the wind in her face and hair. Her hat whipped from her head and hung behind, held by the straps. She could not think straight, could not think of anything, only of that lonely figure on the porch and his two children. And, perversely, she felt insanely jealous of the woman Caleb Blood had married and who had borne his children.

'Caleb Blood!' she called out and his name was whipped away in the wind as she fled from the phantoms of the past.

27

'I'm gonna kill that filthy creature.'

'It beats me how you missed him and not only that but he managed to crease you with a bullet. Maybe he's not such a pushover as we first thought. When we go after him again we'll have to be doubly sure we don't make the same mistake.'

'What about Miss Laura? She seemed pretty riled up over it.'

'Don't worry about Laura. She's just a girl, albeit a girl with a very wealthy father. I'll bring her round. I'm wondering if we should enlist Houseman's help with that squatter. After all, it's not in his interest to have squatters moving in so close to his range. Next thing he'll be missing calves. They're like vermin, spreading crime and disorder wherever they settle.'

'I don't need no help with that piece

of shit. This is personal. No one lays a bullet on me and lives to boast about it.

'Nevertheless, I'll have a word with Houseman. Maybe he knows who that squatter is.'

Mitchell Houseman listened to Kurt Wyman as his guest told him an edited version of the incident with the squatter. The rancher's face creased as his frown deepened.

'A squatter, you say, and opened fire on you. Hell's bells, that place is supposed to be empty. What'd he look like, this fella?' The description of the squatter caused Houseman's concern to deepen. 'If my instincts are right that ain't no squatter but a no-account nuisance as come in here to create bother for us all.' He went to the door of his drawing room and called out instructions to one of the servants. 'Fetch Hecht if he's still around. My foreman had trouble in town with a fella called Caleb Blood. His brother owned that ranch but he's dead now. What about Laura, is she all right?'

'Sure,' Wyman answered smoothly. 'She was mad as hell about it all. She rode off in a fury. I thought she'd be home afore us.'

'Did she talk to this fella?'

'Nah. He weren't in the mood for talking, just shooting.'

When Hecht arrived Wyman was curious about the foreman's injuries but made no comment. He repeated what he had told Houseman about the squatter at the Blood ranch.

'Afore we could talk he opened up with a rifle. Creased Harper. Only Harper was fast enough to put a cylinder of slugs in the doorway to keep his head down while we managed to ride away.'

'That's him all right,' Hecht confirmed. 'Filthy bastard did the same to me. Jumped my men and me without warning, shot Hawkins, and when the sheriff tried to arrest him he killed him also. He's a wild dog gone mad as needs to be put down.'

Afterwards when he was alone with

Harper, Wyman was pensive.

'What is it, Kurt? I know when you're cooking up something or something is bothering you. Don't worry; I can take care of this Blood fella. He was lucky, is all, this morning.'

'As you know there's a railroad coming through here. I've seen the plans. That line runs right along the edge of the Blood ranch. I need to buy up that ranch for my stockholders and I need to buy it up cheap. That's why Blood has to go. I must admit I panicked when I found the place occupied. I was reliably informed it was cleared out. The sheriff that Blood killed was under orders to clear the way for me to buy it. It looks like he failed in his task. Now we have to do it.'

Harper smiled thinly. 'Consider it done, boss.'

'No mistakes this time, Duane. There's a fortune riding on this scheme and I want big slice of it.'

'What about Houseman? You think he'll give you anything when you marry his daughter?'

It was Wyman's turn to smile a cold thin smile. 'I have a bad feeling about Laura's father. He don't look too healthy to me. Maybe he won't survive much beyond the wedding.'

Duane Harper's smile broke into open laughter. 'You're one scheming son of a bitch, Kurt. I think that's why we work so well together. We're two of a kind.'

* * *

It was late when Laura Houseman returned to the Box MH. Her father and mother were waiting for her.

'Thank goodness you are safe, my dear. You had us worried. We . . . we heard as that killer, Caleb Blood, had returned. Kurt said he shot at them.'

Laura's face was tight as she stared at her parents. 'I suppose Kurt told you all about it?'

'Yes, it was a miracle none of you was killed or badly injured by that madman.'

'I don't want to talk about it. I'm tired. I'd just like to go to my room. Goodnight.'

Her parents watched her go with their concern showing plainly on their faces.

'I don't think there's anything to worry about, Alice. From all that's happened Laura will realize what a foul brute that Caleb Blood is. You were foolish to worry about Laura and him meeting again.'

'I'm sure you're right, Mitchell. If my reading of this is right she'll steer clear of that brute from now on.'

28

Laura Houseman could not rid herself of the image of Caleb Blood, as he had stood immobile at the ranch like a tree that had been battered by life but was defying the forces of nature by remaining upright. She was convinced he had known her all along but had not acknowledged her existence and she wondered, was his sighting of her as troubling to him as was her meeting him? Her thoughts were interrupted by a discreet knock on the door.

'Who is it?'

'Kurt, I wanted to see you. Make sure you were all right. Can I come in?'

Reluctantly she opened the door to her fiancé. She stepped back into her room and waited for him to speak.

'I wanted to reassure myself you were all right.'

He moved closer. She waited, making

no movement towards him or any gesture of encouragement.

'This afternoon was a tragic mistake. Duane was out of order opening fire like that and I've reprimanded him. He genuinely thought that squatter was about to open fire. His only thought was for your safety. He thought to forestall any action by the fella and injury to yourself.'

She said nothing, remembering Kurt's provoking of Caleb and the sudden shout. It was the same tactic he had used during the stagecoach robbery. The sudden yell to distract attention away from Harper towards himself, giving the gunman an opportunity to pull his weapon.

'*I'm talking to you, boy!*' Kurt had shouted and Caleb was falling back inside as the bullets hammered into the doorway.

Still she said nothing, waited. Kurt moved closer to her and put out his hands to draw her close. She stepped back.

'Please, Kurt, I'm very tired. We'll talk about this in the morning.'

For a moment she saw a hardening of his features and a dark flare of anger in his eyes, then it was gone. His smile was slightly strained as he nodded.

'Of course, my dear Laura. Or perhaps it would be as well to forget this afternoon. We'll go riding again tomorrow, just you and me. We'll leave Duane behind.'

She said nothing, willing him to go, and he left with a reassuring smile.

'Good night, Laura. I thought you were magnificent this afternoon when you lambasted Duane and myself. You look so imperious when you're angry; imperious and wildly beautiful.'

Then he was gone, leaving her unsettled and uneasy. She could not sleep but tossed and turned and, no matter what she did, the image of Caleb Blood as he had stood today at his ranch was intermingled with the old Caleb she had known previously.

He had such beautiful dark eyes that

sparkled when he laughed. She remembered running her fingers along his fine
jaw-line, lean and tanned and so
handsome. What had happened to turn
him into the ragged creature she had
seen today? And what was his wife like?
He had two children, a boy and a girl.
She tossed and turned as an insane
jealousy tortured her.

'I am engaged to a fine man,' she said
out loud into the room. 'Kurt Wyman
will make a wonderful husband.'

She shivered as she remembered the
burst of anger she had seen in his face
when she spurned him tonight? What
was he really like, this sophisticated
businessman?

'*I'm talking to you, boy!*' Kurt had
shouted and it was the signal for
Harper to pull his gun and start
shooting.

Her thoughts were hot and feverish.
She tossed and turned in the bed,
restless beyond endurance. She knew
what was required. A night ride. That
was what she had done in the past.

Sneaking out at night for a lover's tryst. Caleb laughing, his eyes sparkling in the moonlight and telling her she would get them both into trouble but not meaning any of it, just glad she was there with him and . . .

She was out of bed and getting dressed, the fever of wanting hot inside. There was no way she could help herself. She knew it was madness but she had to see him and put the past to rest once and for all. He would be smelly and revolting and coarse and she would feel disgusted by his crudeness and the fever that burned her up would be assuaged.

The ranch was in darkness. She sat her horse and watched. Nothing stirred in the night. Somewhere in the distance a coyote barked. There was an answering bark much nearer. Were the coyotes hunting or, and the thought came unbidden, were they calling for a mate? She felt ashamed and foolish and resolved to turn around and ride home again. And then the figure loomed out of the darkness and she saw the barrel of a rifle pointing. She froze.

★ ★ ★

Caleb led her horse back into the shadow of the small group of trees growing near the house. He set his rifle down, tethered the horse, and waited.

'You could help a girl down from her horse,' she pouted.

'I remember a time when you didn't need no help.'

There was no give in him. As she slid from her mount she could sense the stiffness in him.

'What are you doing riding around at night?' he asked.

'I could ask you the same. Why are you wandering around out here?'

'Since I returned, twice now someone has tried to kill me. I want to die in my bed but not prematurely.'

'Is that what you are doing — patrolling?'

'I never wanted to come back to the

ranch, but they killed Charlie and I have to set his affairs to rights.'

'Caleb, I'm sorry about Charlie. I heard.' She tried to see his face but it was hopeless with the hair hanging down and the bad light. 'Did they find out who killed him?'

'I'm pretty sure it was Mathew Hecht, him and two others.'

'Hecht! But are you sure?'

'Yeah, he all but admitted to it when he tried to put the blame on two of your father's men.'

She weighed up his words. 'You think my father had something to do with this?' She tried to sound angry but failed.

'Charlie bought wire, was going to fence off. Your father threatened him if he went ahead. Charlie ignored the warning. Next thing he was dead.'

'I saw Hecht,' she said at last when it was plain he was not going to answer her question about her father's involvement. 'He was pretty badly beat up. Was that your doing?'

'That was on the first occasion someone tried to kill me. You witnessed the second attempt.'

She was silent, not knowing how to respond. He sounded so remote, as though he was talking to a stranger, and perhaps that was what she had become. Then he grabbed her and pulled her close. For an insane moment she thought he was going to kiss her and she felt frightened and excited at the same time.

'Stay here,' he whispered. 'Don't come out no matter what.'

Then he was gone leaving her dizzy and agitated by the nearness of his body when he had grabbed her.

29

The four men spread out, coming at the house from different directions. Len Jackson had followed the wagon and when he returned the outlaws had decided to act immediately.

'It would be hard to take him during the day. He would see us coming. I reckon we go in tonight and catch him while he's sleeping. We could set fire to the place and shoot him when he comes running out.'

'That's no good,' Hardy growled. 'If he has that reward money in the house it might get burned up. No, we stalk him. Lure him out and then kill him. We can search for the money at our leisure.'

'He has those kids with him. You know, the ones we picked up accidental when we stole that wagon.'

Hardy shrugged. 'The hell with the

kids! They won't cause us any bother. It's Blood we're after and I want to do the killing. If we can take him alive so much the better. We can make him talk and tell us where the reward money is. But he's a rattlesnake. Don't take any chances. Shoot first and ask questions after. If we have bother finding the cash those kids probably know something.'

The house was quiet and dark. The outlaws imagined the man they were after to be sound asleep in the house. The plan was to lure him out into the open. Broody was to go for the horses and make as if he were stealing them. When Blood came out to deal with the rustlers the rest of the gang would be lying in wait and take him.

Len Jackson heard movement out on his left flank.

'Is that you, Hardy? You should be round the other side.'

There was a grunt and he assumed Hardy would take the hint and move away. Then something reared up beside him — the figure of a man. Too late, he noticed the long lank hair hanging in tails around the man's head.

'Hell . . . '

He tried to bring his gun to bear. Something hard and brutal hit him on the temple. It crushed the frontal part of the skull, driving splinters of bone into the outlaw's brain. He dropped, making no more noise than a rabbit falling to the earth under a hunter's rifle. That was what Caleb Blood had used to kill him — using his rifle as a club.

Caleb the hunter stood over the man, waiting to make sure he was out of the fight. He had learned a useful name before he had struck the man with his rifle butt.

Hardy!

He went to ground again, stalking the men who had come in the night to ambush him. A commotion in the corral started up. He ignored the obvious attempt to lure the inhabitants of the house outside.

During the war he had stalked men,

being sent at night to spy out enemy positions. His task was to create terror and panic amongst the enemy troops by silent night-stalking and killing sentries and destroying outposts. He was good at it, often staying out all night and coming back exhausted and bloody with killing.

His keen senses detected the smell of tobacco. It was not active tobacco, just the body odour of a man who was a user.

'Hardy?' he hissed.

'Naw, it's Vance. Who's that?'

'Has he come out yet?'

'No sign yet. You should be over there.'

Caleb could see the dark outline now of a man crouching within the vegetable patch, the tall weeds giving some cover from observation.

'Get back to your position!'

'Sorry.'

'Wait, you're not — '

Caleb fired then, not risking coming to grips with the man. He fired two shots into the head, wanting to make sure the man was dead.

'Yippee! You got him, boys.' The yell came from the man causing the distraction with the horses.

'I got him!' Caleb yelled in reply and dropped to the dirt. He lay flat, waiting, all his senses alert. He watched for the man coming around the house from the direction of the corral, sighted on him, watched the shadowy figure for a brief moment, then pulled the trigger. There was a sudden faltering in the running man's gait.

'Hell . . . ' the cry came faintly through the night air.

Caleb fired again and the figure by the house went over backwards. Caleb stayed where he was and waited, not knowing how many more he had to contend with, listening to the night sounds, trying to distinguish the natural from the unnatural. He was not worried about the children inside. All the doors and windows were secure and he had instructed them not to come out no matter what.

'I'll be outside watching the house, so you'll be quite safe as long as you stay inside.'

Then came the scream. Caleb's head jerked up. It came from the direction of the trees where he had left Laura. A cold feeling of dread started and he slowly sat up, watching for anything that would give him an indication where the night raiders might be lying, waiting for him to expose himself.

'Blood, I got your woman here!'

Caleb stared towards the trees. It was impossible to make out anything in the shadows.

'Vance, where are you?' the man in the trees called.

A heavy silence stretched over everything.

'Jackson, Broody are you there?'

Still that ominous silence reigned over the night.

Caleb listened hard. No more names were called out. He had downed three men. The man in the trees had called out three names. That meant only one thing. He had disposed of the team of raiders and only one was left.

He began worming his way in the direction of the trees. Even as he began to move there came the sound of flesh hitting flesh.

'Tell him, you bitch! Tell him you're here with me.'

'Go to hell . . . ' Her voice was cut of by the sound of another slap.

'You hear, Blood. Your woman is dead unless you come out with your hands held high and no weapons.'

'What sort of a deal is that? I stand up and you shoot me and then you shoot the woman as well. Why did you come here anyway? Did Houseman hire you?' Even as he said it he regretted it.

'No one hired us. We just want what's owed us.'

Caleb thought about this, tried to fathom what was meant but could make no sense of it.

'What is it you are owed?'

'The reward money. You got five thousand dollars from the bank. That was our gold you took. We want the reward they gave you.'

It was becoming clear. He had thought Harwinton and his cronies he had found at the outlaw camp were all of the gang. Now their companions were coming for revenge. He knew that whatever happened this Hardy would kill him, and possibly Laura would die too. He cursed the chance that had brought her into this danger.

'You can have the money. Just let the woman go free.'

'All in good time. You go in the house and bring out the money. Once that's in my mitt I ride outta here. Then we're quits.'

Caleb stood up. He knew he was risking a shot from the trees but he had to gamble a lot now if he was to come out of this with a whole skin and Laura unharmed.

'I'll get you the money. It's in the house.'

A shape emerged from under the trees. He could see the smaller figure of Laura in front of the burly shape of Hardy. Even in the dimness he could see the outline of a revolver pressing against her breast.

'Throw your rifle.'

Caleb raised the rifle and tossed it into the weeds.

'Now your handgun.'

'I ain't got one.'

'You better not try anything. This revolver is primed and ready to go off. Any tricks and this little lady will have a slug lodged in her heart. Ain't no one ever recovered from that afore.'

'Don't do anything stupid. I'll get the money.'

He turned to the house and began walking, any moment expecting a shot in the back, but none came and he reached the front door safely. Inside he could see the children peering out from their bedroom. He talked to them as he made his preparations.

'If anything happens to me run out

back and hide. Wait till someone comes for you.'

The gunnysack was filled now. He returned outside.

'Here it is,' he called holding the sack high in the air.

'Walk over here slow and careful. You stumble or make a false move and your woman is dead.'

'I just want her safe, that's all.'

He began walking. Hardy and his captive waited by the trees. It was still dark, the only illumination the stars bathing everything in an eerie bluish light.

Hardy was going to kill him and Laura. Caleb was aware of this fact. The outlaw was a ruthless killer. He would want revenge against Caleb, for it looked as though he had wiped out most of the gang that had raided the bank that day in Musgrave. He walked until only a few paces separated him from the gunman and his captive.

'Stop. Turn around slow.'

'So's you can shoot me in the back.

Look, I got the money as you asked. I'll show you.'

Caleb's hand was inside the gunny-sack, his hand closing over the butt of the gun. The first shot smashed the gunman's elbow, the heavy slug severing muscle and tissue. Hardy screamed as the hand that held the gun was rendered useless. The second shot took out his eye and he was staggering back. Laura fell forward. Caleb put another bullet into the outlaw's head. He knew it wasn't necessary but he wanted to make sure.

30

Once more they were travelling in the wagon, Caleb senior, Caleb junior and Gale. Laura Houseman was with them, riding alongside on her horse. Caleb would not allow her to travel back alone to her home.

'Come morning, I will take the children and ride with you till I know you are safe; then we will continue on into Newtown. I have to inform Deputy Hardin of the attack on the ranch.'

But Laura did not want to go home, not just yet anyway. Meeting Caleb had thrown her emotions into turmoil. She needed time to sort out her feelings.

'I shall ride into town with you. You will need a witness as to what happened. I can vouch that everything you did was in self-defence.'

It was not what he had wanted. There were enough complications in his life without more. Reluctantly he had agreed.

It was still early when they rode into town. Only a few traders were about, opening up stores and offices ready for the day's business. There was no one at the jailhouse and the little party drove over to the hotel.

'Mr Blood!'

The last time Caleb had seen the hotel manager the man had been lying behind his desk in a dead faint. Now he stared apprehensively at Caleb as if he expected him to start a fight in the lobby of the hotel.

'Can I order breakfast for four?'

Caleb turned and raised an eyebrow at Laura. She nodded her acceptance of the invitation to breakfast with them. The manager was shaking his head nervously.

'I'm sorry, there are no vacancies,' he stammered.

Caleb made no response but stood motionless waiting. It was embarrassing watching the man squirm before

Caleb's stoic silence.

'No . . . no . . . vacancies . . . '

Laura stepped forward. 'Excuse me Mr — what is your name?'

'Belfrage . . . Terrill Belfrage, ma'am.'

'My name is Laura Houseman, daughter of Mitchell Houseman, the owner of Box MH. I need a meal and a room for this family.' She spoke her request quietly but authoritatively.

Belfrage's eyes widened. 'Miss . . . Miss Houseman . . . just a minute.' His hands, shaking a little, were turning pages in the hotel register. 'Ah . . . yes, yes, I see there is a vacancy after all. How silly of me.'

By now Caleb was walking away, leaving Laura to complete the transaction.

Over breakfast Caleb realized he did not want to leave the youngsters on their own while he went to report to Deputy Hardin.

'Miss Houseman, if you aren't in a hurry to get back home would it be possible to keep an eye on Gale and

Caleb while I complete my business in town?'

'The name is Laura, or had you forgotten.'

He looked away from her and stared off into the distance, not wanting her to see the expression in his eyes. She waited patiently and he realized she would not give him an answer until he acknowledged his omission.

'Miss Laura . . . '

'It's Laura, Caleb.'

He still was not looking in her direction. 'Laura,' he mumbled.

'It would be a pleasure to mind the children for you.'

He got up and tossed his napkin on the table. 'You be good for the lady,' he instructed the children, still not looking at Laura. 'I have to go to the bank and the solicitor to sort some things out about the ranch. I may be a while.'

He left them, walking self-consciously from the dining room knowing she would be staring after him. The jailhouse had still not opened and

Caleb went across to the bank. When he identified himself he was invited into the manager's office.

'Mr Blood, it is a pleasure to meet with you. I'm Paul Coles. Mr Starr from the Musgrave bank asked me to extend all courtesy to you in view of the service you rendered to him in recovering the stolen gold. How can I assist you?'

'I believe my brother Charlie left the deeds of his ranch with you as security for some loans he made.'

'That is correct. What happened to your brother was a terrible tragedy. Our law officers seemed unable to track down the killers. However, since your coming into Newtown I believe that omission has been rectified.'

Caleb looked shrewdly at the bank manager. 'News certainly gets around fast. When I came to Newtown it was to settle up Charlie's affairs. It was not my intention to seek revenge for his murder, but his killers obviously thought otherwise and they came after me.

Sheriff LeMoyne made an attempt on my life. I carry a bullet hole in my shoulder from his gun. I had to kill the sheriff to prevent him from killing me.'

'Mr Blood, you don't have to justify yourself to me. Fortunately for you Deputy Hardin witnessed the whole affair and has told his tale to all who will listen. No one holds you responsible for the killing. It was justified self-defence. Now, how can I be of service?'

'When I recovered Mr Starr's gold I received a substantial reward. I would like to use part of that money to buy back Charlie's deeds.'

'That may not be necessary, Mr Blood. There are a number of parties interested in purchasing the ranch. You would have no problem selling up and the notes outstanding would be absorbed in the purchase price.'

Caleb frowned. 'Are you sure? The ranch never was very profitable. Charlie struggled to make a go of it. That's why he had to borrow from you. Who would want to buy an outfit teetering on the edge?

Coles pulled a folder from a drawer in his desk and studied a sheet of paper before replying. 'A local rancher, Mr Houseman, is one prospective buyer. There is another potential purchaser — a company from the East.'

'What's their interest in the ranch?'

Coles did not answer immediately and appeared to be studying the papers in front of him. Caleb waited patiently. At last the bank manager looked up.

'This is privileged information, Mr Blood. If it were anyone other than you I would not divulge what I know. East-West Construction's main interests are building railroads. I can disclose nothing else. I shouldn't even have told you the identity of the company, never mind what they do.'

'East-West Construction,' Caleb repeated. He remembered Laura letting slip that her fiancé was connected to the same company. 'Would that be a certain Kurt Wyman?'

'I see you are better informed than I thought.' Coles eyed Caleb shrewdly. 'Whatever happens, none of this came from me, though if I read you right you are not the sort of man to run off at the mouth.'

Caleb nodded thoughtfully but said nothing further.

'In the light of what you now know, Mr Blood, what do you wish me to do?'

'Have the money transferred and clear off the debt on the ranch. In the meantime I have much to think on. When I came back to Newtown I had thought to settle Charlie's debts and sell the ranch. If I put the sale money with the reward I got for saving the bank it would amount to a tidy sum. My intention was to put this combined sum in a trust for Charlie's children and that would give them a good start in life. I'm wondering what East-West Construction see in Charlie's ranch. My instincts tell me no company would invest in a run-down ranch unless they could see a big return for their investment.

'I'm obliged to you for all your help. And you don't need to worry, what has passed between us here today stays between us.'

31

Caleb walked across to the Sunshine café and ordered a coffee. In the light of what he had learned at the bank his plans were all thrown askew and he needed to think things over.

As he told Coles, he had intended to combine all the cash and put it in a trust for the children. With their financial future secure he would find a good family to take in Gale and Caleb and give them a sheltered and loving upbringing.

His own future was a blank, which did not bother him unduly. He had drifted for so long he imagined that pattern would continue.

So engrossed in his thoughts was he that he was not aware of the customers coming and going for breakfasts and drinks in the café until a tray was set down opposite him. Annoyed, he looked up into the chubby face of Deputy Hardin.

'Morning, I hope you don't mind me joining you.' Without waiting for a reply the fat man eased himself into the chair and sighed gustily. 'A man should start the day on a full belly.'

Hardin's idea of a full belly was a plate heaped with eggs and rashers of bacon along with a side dish stacked with biscuits and a jug of molasses accompanied by a pot of coffee. He diligently went to work with his knife and fork. Caleb watched fascinated as the deputy scooped up forkfuls of eggs and bacon and crammed them in his mouth.

'I see you been busy again shooting up people,' Hardin said, giving Caleb a view of mashed food inside his mouth as he spoke. 'I guess you're the sorta fella as trouble follows you around.' He suddenly giggled, spraying bits of egg back on the table. 'I guess I'm taking a risk sitting here with you. Any minute now there'll be a bank robbery or a shoot-out or a stampede of cattle through the town.'

The food on his plate was disappearing at a bewildering rate.

'You know about that?' Caleb said, puzzled the deputy knew about the attack on the ranch by the outlaws. 'Have you spoken to Miss Houseman.'

Hardin's eyebrows elevated. 'Miss Houseman? Nah, fella name of Wyman came by to make a complaint against you. Claimed you tried to kill him. Said you winged his employee, Harper, during the attack. Wanted me to arrest you and sling you in jail on a charge of attempted murder.'

The pile of food was almost devoured. Hardin took a biscuit and used it to wipe up the greasy remnants of egg. He refilled his coffee mug and offered Caleb a top-up. Then he started on the plate of biscuits, covering each with a liberal dose of molasses.

'You gonna arrest me, then?'

'Help yourself to a biscuit.'

The plate of biscuits was emptying at

the rate of one per bite. Hardin pushed a biscuit in, his jaws convulsed a couple of times and he was ready for the next.

'You ever think of entering an eating contest, Deputy?' Caleb asked.

Hardin laughed out loud, spraying crumbs. 'I just like eating. Some men like to gamble or drink liquor or go with women. Me, I just like a good feed.'

Caleb was chastened as he remembered his own addiction to whiskey. 'You ain't answered my question. Are you gonna arrest me?'

Hardin took a swig of coffee to wash down the last of the biscuits. He broke wind with a contented look on his face.

'Just as I am a connoisseur of good food I also consider myself an excellent judge of men. Wyman buttonholed me this morning afore I even had my breakfast. That don't sit right for a start. I took an instant dislike to the man.

'When I had a good look at his pardner, Harper, the fella as you winged, I saw gunslinger writ large as a store sign. He had the look of a man who is fast and deadly just the same way a rattlesnake is. If he's gunning for you I'd advise you hightail it outta town fast. I'd like to know how you managed to put a slug in him. But then again, mebby you're a wee bit deadly yourself. The other day I saw four men try to put you down. You killed two and laid the other two out.'

'I will have that refill after all.'

Caleb reached out, took the deputy's coffee pot and poured. They sat in silence for a moment.

'I don't figger you, Deputy Hardin. I shot your sheriff and Houseman's ranch hand. Now you got a complaint from this Wyman that I tried to kill him. Yet you don't make a move against me.'

'Like I say, I consider myself a good judge of men. Sheriff LeMoyne was a mean bastard. I watched him stalk you and when you looked like you were getting the best of Hecht and his cowboys he took a shot at you. Only you got lucky and downed him or it would be you lying down in the morgue. So just you tell me what happened between you and Harper.'

Caleb told him how the men had ridden up with Miss Houseman and, with her watching, tried to shoot him. Hardin was nodding.

'You're saying Miss Houseman will vouch for the facts?'

'Deputy, there's more.'

'More what?'

'More trouble, more shooting. Last night four men came out to my ranch after me.' Caleb paused.

There was a bemused look on the deputy's face as he sat regarding the man opposite.

'Go on.'

'They were the rest of the gang as I took the gold from. I thought I had finished them all. In that I was mistaken. They came hunting me last night.' Again Caleb paused in his narrative.

'Where are they now?'

'In the woodshed back at Charlie's ranch.'

'You locked them in there?'

'I didn't need to lock them in. They're not going anywhere.'

Deputy Hardin hooted and slapped the table at the same time. 'Goddamn it, Caleb Blood, you're a one-man, walking, shooting army.'

Caleb blinked, uncertain, not knowing how to interpret the deputy's reaction.

'Goddamn it, I'll send someone out to collect the bodies. Outlaws, you say. There's probably a reward for them owlhoots. I'll make sure it's paid out to you. Well, goddamn my soul. Caleb Blood, if you don't take the biscuit!'

'Reward!' The possibility of a reward had never occurred to Caleb. 'Maybe you could send the money to Musgrave. Those outlaws killed some folk when they hit the bank. It seems fitten if the money went to their dependants.'

Deputy Hardin said nothing, sipping

his mug of coffee and just gazing at Caleb.

'Am I free to go?' Caleb asked at last.

'Hardin and Wyman are still in town. They're killers, them two. Just you watch your back, young 'un. When I asked them where they would be staying if I needed to consult them they told me the hotel. Wyman has a room booked. When he told me the room number so as I could contact him I specifically remember it's on the front looking down into the street.'

The two men sat facing each other. There was a slight smile on the deputy's face.

'Thanks,' Caleb said at last. 'Can I pay for your breakfast?'

'Nope, but if you're still around tonight you could buy me dinner.'

32

Laura Houseman was in a quandary. Her expensive schooling at the academy had not prepared her for taking care of children. Once they had settled in the hotel room she was at a loss how to entertain her young charges. The only skill she could call upon that might be of help was reading.

'Children, I need you to be very good while I go and borrow a book. When I return I'll read you a story.'

Then she wondered whether her idea was necessary. The children looked worn out. The disturbed night and the early morning ride into town had taken their toll. Their eyelids were drooping and Gale yawned, sparking a similar response in her brother. Laura made them lie on top of the bed and threw a coverlet over them. They smiled wanly at her before falling asleep almost instantly.

Tiptoeing to the door she opened it cautiously, anxious not to disturb the sleeping children. She paused in the doorway and looked back at the bed. All seemed peaceful, then she heard voices in the hallway. There was something familiar about those voices and she peered through the partly open door.

Kurt Wyman and Duane Harper were standing in the corridor deep in conversation. Laura was not quite ready to confront her fiancé and she stepped back inside the room.

In a while the voices ceased and she heard a door close. Only then did she venture out. When she descended the stairs she could see Duane Harper with Terrill Belfrage, the manager. Harper had his back to her and she managed to slip out unnoticed.

Laura headed for the church. Mrs Lansdowne, the preacher's wife, had an extensive library and she hoped to borrow something suitable from her.

'*The Adventures of Huckleberry Finn*,' the preacher's wife advised. 'The reverend doesn't approve of it but I see no harm in the tale.'

When Laura stepped out of the church she noticed a man in the cemetery. There was something familiar in the ragged appearance of the figure that quickened her heartbeat. She walked up into the graveyard and saw Caleb squatting by a grave that, from the raw earth, looked as if it was a recent interment. Her steps slowed as she approached. He looked up at her but remained squatting by the grave.

'Caleb.'

He nodded his head in acknowledgment but did not speak. She read the inscription and confirmed her notion this was the grave of Charlie and Elvira Blood.

'Where are the children?'

'I left them asleep at the hotel. I came down here to get a book so as I could read to them when they awoke.'

'Charlie asked me once what it was

like in the war. I never told him but the truth is they made me into an assassin. I went out into the field and slaughtered men and boys, just like myself, who did not understand what it was we were doing. My soul was sick with the butchery. I never wanted to pick up gun or knife again.' As he spoke Caleb traced patterns on the soil with his finger. 'When I left the army after the war I thought I had done with killing. When Mathew Hecht ordered me outta Newtown I knew if I did not go I would have to kill him. So I ran away and instead Hecht killed Charlie.

'I had a friend, Marty Sandford. He owned a livery stable in Musgrave. He told me he was gonna give me a job even though he was barely making a living. Raiders came into town and Marty took up his old rifle and went out and got himself killed while I slept in his livery. The raiders then went on to kill Elvira. I know she was dying anyway, but they shot her like you would a dog in the street. They kidnapped Gale and Caleb. And all this while I was hiding in Marty's livery.

'Last night, four outlaws came after me. They were the remnants of the gang that shot Marty and Elvira. They were coming for revenge. I had Charlie's children to protect and then you came along and that made the thing even more fraught. In that case there was no choice, it was kill or be killed. Now there are more men in the town gunning for me. It seems to me I can't run away. Every time I chicken out someone close to me gets killed or hurt.'

Though she guessed the answer she still had to ask, 'Who is after you, Caleb?'

He did not respond and she knelt on the ground opposite him with the grave between them.

'My parents sent me to Philadelphia to be educated. I believe now it was to keep us apart. I thought I had forgotten you, Caleb. I was all set to marry Kurt but now I don't know what I want.

Since coming back I am all confused.'

'I did my best to forget you.'

A silence settled between them. In the background could be heard the noise of the town going about the business of the day. Vehicles trundled through the streets and men called out greetings. Deep in the cemetery a songbird trilled out a lively tune that seemed out of keeping amongst this place of the dead.

'At the academy I studied Shakespeare, the great English playwright. There was one of his plays I struggled to understand: *Troilus and Cressida*.' She looked at him and could see he was watching her, waiting. 'The play never made sense to me. Cressida and Troilus were lovers living in Troy at the time the Greeks laid siege to the city. Cressida was taken from Troilus and sent into the Greek camp as ransom for a Trojan general. She had no say in the matter. She was but a piece of merchandise in the affairs of men who were only interested in power and conquest.

'My parents sent me away to separate me from you. I was to be educated and made fit for a more suitable husband, someone with power and wealth.'

'What happened to her, Cressida I mean?'

'In order to survive she had to forget Troilus and make the best of a bad situation. What I understand now is that Cressida had no say in her fate. There was no man to speak up for her or protect her.'

He was silent, thinking over her story. 'What are you saying?' he asked eventually after a long pause.

'Cressida had nowhere to go, no one to help her. It is a man's world. The men in a family decide the woman's fate; whom she marries, what she does with her life. Last night when that dreadful man held a gun on me, there was only one person who could help me. Though I was frightened I did not panic for I knew there was someone I could depend on.'

His finger went on tracing in the dirt

meaningless, meandering lines and scrawls.

'They want Charlie's ranch. It's something to do with the railroad coming through here. I suspect that's why Charlie was killed. That's why they have been trying to kill me. Once I'm out of the way I fear for Charlie's children. I have to do this thing, Laura. Please go back to Gale and Caleb and mind them while I do what has to be done.'

'Kurt and Harper are down at the hotel. It is my belief they are lying in wait for you.'

He bowed his head. 'So be it,' he said, his voice barely audible.

33

He made his way to the wagon, reached into the trunk for the gun rig and belted it around his waist. Though he had checked the loads and mechanism when he placed the weapon there this morning before coming into town he tested everything once more. Then he looked back up towards the church and cemetery where his brother was buried.

'When does the killing stop, Charlie? Maybe it only ends when I'm up there in boot hill with you and Elvira.'

He started walking down the street, keeping to the side opposite the hotel. He knew enough not to let the killers place him with his back to the hotel.

The town seemed just as usual as he walked. Traffic moved in an even flow along both sides of the street with drivers and pedestrians calling greetings and all seemingly engrossed in the business of the day. When he stopped walking he was directly across from the entrance to the hotel.

A figure was lounging on a rocker placed on the boardwalk out front. Caleb recognized Duane Harper, but made no move towards the gunman, just stood there waiting.

Without raising his head he let his eyes stray to the windows above the entrance. One window was open, the bottom section pulled up as if to air the room. The lace curtains fluttered gently in a slight breeze. It was not possible to see into the room, nor could he discern whether anyone was lurking within. Indolently he leaned against the upright supporting the veranda that sheltered the boardwalk and settled down to wait. He was expert at this waiting game.

After the traumatic parting from Harwinton, Caleb had ended up at a recruiting station. When he told the officer he had ridden with Harwinton he was assigned to a special unit.

A band of men were being signed up

for guerrilla warfare. In the course of a few months Caleb was trained to infiltrate enemy lines and commit acts of sabotage. He was sent out at night to reconnoitre the positions of the Confederate troops and, where possible, silence their sentries.

Part of the skills of successful night work was the ability to remain invisible, sometimes only yards from the enemy. It required patience and immobility at times for prolonged periods. Now he stood only a road's width from the men who were determined to kill him. His old skills were invaluable now. He was like the column of wood against which he leaned, motionless but, unlike the pillar, all his senses were alert.

Behind him he heard the clatter of ladies' boots as their voices approached and passed him by. A workman was hammering at some task and whistling at the same time. It seemed to him people were going about their business without a care in the world.

A great sadness welled up in him. He

thought of Charlie's children sleeping upstairs in the same hotel where death awaited him and the sadness turned to anger. Gale and Caleb's lives had been blighted by the greed of covetous men, their parents murdered and they themselves terrorized.

Inevitably his thoughts turned to Laura and her telling him of the Shakespeare play. Laura claimed Cressida had no man to protect her. While he pondered over her conversation with him in the cemetery he thought he knew why Laura had told him that tale.

As he wondered at the things that came into his mind with these recollections the sadness fell away, to be replaced by anger. It was not a hot anger but a cold anger tracking through him like iced water. He became composed and focused and just then his waiting was over, for across the road he saw Harper get up from his rocker and stare across at him. His waiting game had paid off and it looked as though the enemy was keen to make the first move.

* ★ ★

Laura Houseman made sure the children were still sleeping and, leaving the borrowed book in the room, made her way downstairs to the lobby. Immediately she could see Duane Harper seated on the veranda.

'Miss Houseman.'

The voice behind her startled her and she whirled around to see who had spoken. Terrill Belfrage, the hotel manager, was smiling politely at her.

'Can I get you anything, Miss Houseman?'

Laura wanted nothing but to stop the violence that was about to erupt out in the street, but she knew she was powerless to intervene. For a moment she was nonplussed, for she needed an excuse to stay in the lobby and watch events from there.

'Tea, if you have any.'

'Of course, I'll have it brought in presently. Will anyone be joining you?'

'No. I will take tea alone.'

Back East she had acquired the habit of tea drinking. Now she was glad of the excuse it gave her to stay.

The lobby was furnished with comfortable leather-covered armchairs and she chose a seat that gave her a view of the door and the roadway outside. She could not see Harper from this viewpoint, for he was seated to one side of the doorway.

When she sat down she shivered as if from cold, yet the interior of the hotel was pleasantly warm. She hunched in the chair trembling, and fear, like an awful malady, grew inside her quivering body.

While she sat and waited she was remembering the deadliness of the two men pitched against Caleb. She had witnessed their lethal efficiency when the stagecoach was held up. Somehow that dangerous combination had not worked when they tried on that first occasion to kill Caleb at the ranch house. As she mulled over the chances of Caleb surviving she began to see a way of helping even out his chances.

The tea arrived served on a silver tray and Laura poured. Her hand was trembling but inside she was calm.

34

'Blood!'

Caleb did not move from his nonchalant stance on the boardwalk.

'Caleb Blood, I'm talking to you! I'm calling you out.'

Still Caleb made no response. He had deliberately chosen his spot. The upright he was leaning against was about a foot thick and, if necessary, would give him a margin of cover when the action started.

Duane Harper stepped out into the roadway. He had removed his jacket and Caleb could see the gun high on his hip, set for a cross draw. Now that the encounter had kicked off he was very calm — icy calm. It was dangerous territory he was moving into. His attention was on Harper but another part of his brain was very much aware of the window with the flapping curtains.

People were beginning to take notice, realizing that something momentous was happening. Harper stood alone on the street and there was a palpable air of menace from the man.

'What are you, yalla, Blood? I hear tell you're a yalla dog. Come down here in the street and face me like a man.'

Caleb stopped leaning against the upright and straightened up. His hand hung low over his gun butt. Harper would be fast, deadly fast. But he also had a back-up plan to make sure of killing his victim. Kurt Wyman was up in the hotel room, maybe even now lining up his gun on Caleb.

Suddenly Caleb thought of Charlie, and Elvira finding him by the broken fence. He didn't know whether Wyman had ordered the killing but he had a shrewd idea this thing went further back than the harassment of the past few days.

Elvira had claimed men had come by at night after Charlie's murder and fired shots to frighten the family into giving up the ranch. And they had almost succeeded. Nothing stood in the way of Wyman and the East-West Construction Company taking over Charlie's ranch but two frightened children and a down-and-out saddle tramp.

The curtains fluttered in the breeze but he could not see anything behind them. He couldn't look hard for he had to keep his attention on Harper. Harper was deadly. Caleb sensed the gunman was confident he could take down this raggedy man without his friend's help.

'Come on, yallabelly! You got lucky last time and put a slug in me but you were hiding inside a house that time. Now it's face to face. You and me. It takes a man to do that. Do you want me just to shoot you down like the coyote you are.'

As he called out the insults Harper was moving closer, step by step. Caleb knew it would be soon now, very soon. The curtains fluttered a distraction to his concentration. While he dealt with Harper it gave Wyman an opportunity to put a bullet in him from his vantage point in the window. Caleb needed an edge, but nothing suggested itself.

The street was clearing now as people saw what was happening. They would watch the duel from windows and doorways. When the action was over they would come out in the street and . . .

Two things happened then. Harper went for his gun and someone in the hotel uttered a scream, loud and piercing. Caleb's gun was coming up but Harper fired first and wooden splinters erupted from the upright beside Caleb. Caleb fired a fraction behind Harper and the gunman jerked back as the slug punched him in the abdomen. He backed up a pace or two but Caleb's attention was at the window when the shot whistled beneath his arm and his body. Quickly he stepped behind the splintered upright and, steadying the barrel of his Colt against the post, placed two shots into the glass and one through the open window.

He saw what looked like a shadow in the room and fired again, but the shape was growing more distinct and leaning out against the wrecked frame of the window. A hand holding a gun protruded from the broken glass and Caleb fired again. The outline of a man leaned out through the shattered window at an impossible angle, toppling forward, coming all the way out, glass and wood spilling out and falling to the veranda. Kurt Wyman pitched out the ruined window, tumbling down, his body bouncing off the sloping roof of the veranda, rolling out and dropping lifelessly to the dirt.

Caleb was kneeling behind the upright, his gun trained on Harper. Duane Harper was sitting in the road, his hand pressed against his belly, trying to stem the red tide of crimson spilling through his fingers. His gun lay unheeded beside him.

Slowly Caleb stood and stepped down on the roadway. Harper sensed him coming and looked up, his eyes painfilled and venomous.

'Damn you, Blood . . . '

His hand crabbed towards the gun in the dirt, pulling it into his hand and bringing it up. Caleb squeezed the trigger and froze as he listened to the audible click of the hammer falling on a spent cartridge. Harper was bringing up his weapon.

'I have the last shot, Blood . . . '

Caleb tensed for the gunshot and sensed rather than saw a figure emerge from the hotel. All his attention was focused on the black bore of the gun aimed at him by the wounded Harper.

The shot when it came seemed loud and shocking. Harper jerked to one side as a crimson spray blossomed from his head. Slowly he canted to one side and keeled over to rest in the dirt, the gun in his hand unfired.

Caleb looked beyond the dead man. Laura stood white-faced beside the sprawled figure of her dead fiancé. She was holding Kurt Wyman's gun in both hands with the smoke still curling from the barrel.

People were gathering in the street now the shooting was over. Caleb took the gun from Laura and stuffed it in his waistband.

'Come inside.'

He guided her into the hotel, ignoring the terrified manager cowering behind his desk, and steered her upstairs to the room. They stood inside the door looking at the children still sleeping peacefully. Caleb could feel Laura trembling beside him and reached out to her, unsure whether she would want him to hold her. She moved into his embrace, her arms held tight in front, her hands clasped beneath her chin.

'It was you who screamed?'

Laura's head nodded. 'It was something they did. Kurt would shout and distract everyone while Duane pulled his gun.'

'You saved my life.'

'We're even, then: you saved me.'

Tentatively he held her, feeling her body quivering like a frightened bird in a snare.

'Laura, I been thinking about Cressida. If I had been Troilus I would have gone into the Greek camp after her.'

'Oh, Caleb . . . '

She freed her arms and slid them around his waist, letting her cheek rest against his chest. He held her gently as if afraid she would break in his arms. After a while she spoke.

'If I had been Cressida I would have waited for Troilus to come for me.'

THE END

We do hope that you have enjoyed reading this large print book.

Did you know that all of our titles are available for purchase?

We publish a wide range of high quality large print books including:
Romances, Mysteries, Classics
General Fiction
Non Fiction and Westerns

Special interest titles available in large print are:
The Little Oxford Dictionary
Music Book, Song Book
Hymn Book, Service Book

Also available from us courtesy of Oxford University Press:
Young Readers' Dictionary
(large print edition)
Young Readers' Thesaurus
(large print edition)

For further information or a free brochure, please contact us at:
Ulverscroft Large Print Books Ltd.,
The Green, Bradgate Road, Anstey,
Leicester, LE7 7FU, England.
Tel: (00 44) 0116 236 4325
Fax: (00 44) 0116 234 0205

Other titles in the
Linford Western Library:

HELL FIRE IN PARADISE

Chuck Tyrell

Laurel Baker lost her husband and her two boys on the same day. Then, menacingly, logging magnate Robert Dunn rides into her ranch on Paradise Creek to buy her out. Laurel refuses as her loved ones are buried there — prompting Dunn to try shooting to get his way. Laurel's friends stick by her, but will their loyalty match Dunn's ten deadly gunmen? And in the final battle for her land, can she live through hell fire in Paradise?

THE BLACK MOUNTAIN DUTCHMAN

Steve Ritchie

In Wyoming, when Maggie Buckner is captured by a gang of outlaws, 'the Dutchman' is the only one who can free her. Near Savage Peak, the old man adjusts the sights on his Remington No. 1 rifle as the riders come into range. When he stops shooting, three of the captors lay dead. After striking the first deadly blows, the Dutchman trails the group across South Pass like the fourth horseman of the apocalypse . . . and surely Hell follows with him.

THE FIGHTING MAN

Alan Irwin

Young Rob Sinclair, a homesteader's son in the Wyoming Territory, has never handled a gun. But when the Nolan gang kills his parents, he's determined to bring the culprits to justice. Against the prevailing knowledge that only a real fighting man could defeat the Nolan gang, Rob learns to fight and sets out to search for the killers. He eventually reaches the Texas Panhandle, little knowing what awaits him there. Can he complete such a perilous mission alone?

BLOOD FEUD

John Dyson

Higo, a Japanese railroad worker, kills two guards and escapes into Utah's canyonlands, and when Cal Mitchell goes after him — it's not just for the $500 reward . . . Along with his tempestuous passion for Modesty, dark secrets beckon Cal homeward, towards the mountains of Zion. He also seeks vengeance against the five Granger brothers. Blood flows and bullets fly as Cal steps back into his murky past. Can he find peace when the odds are stacked against him?